MYLOMON

MYLOMON

WARRIORS OF SANGRIN

STARR HUNTRESS
NANCEY CUMMINGS

Mylomon: Warriors of Sangrin
Copyright Nancey Cummings

Cover Design by Nancey Cummings

Published September 2017
Published by Menura Press

Print Edition

Author's Note: This is a work of fiction and all people, places and incidents are products of the author's imagination. All characters depicted in this work of fiction are eighteen years of age or older.

The Story So Far

When aliens arrived on Earth, it happened with an invasion—just like the sci-fi movies taught us to expect.

The vicious Suhlik meant to enslave Earth and rob her of her resources. Only the Mahdfel warriors were able to stand against them.

Once the slaves of the Suhlik, the Mahdfel won their freedom. But as a lingering reminder of their oppression at the hands of the Suhlik they are unable to have female children.

Now, in exchange for the protection of Earth, the hunky alien warriors demand only one price: Every childless, single and otherwise healthy woman on Earth is tested for genetic compatibility for marriage with a Mahdfel warrior. If the match is 98.5% or better, the bride is instantly teleported away to her new mate.

No exceptions.

Mylomon is not a standalone story. It immediately follows the events from *Kalen*. You could read it on its own but you might enjoy the story more having first read *Kalen*.

Are you a
STARR HUNTRESS?

Do you love to read sci fi romance about strong, independent women and the sexy alien males who love them?

Starr Huntress is a coalition of the brightest Starrs in romance banding together to explore uncharted territories.

If you like your men horny—maybe literally— and you're equal opportunity skin color—because who doesn't love a guy with blue or green skin?— then join us as we dive into swashbuckling space adventure, timeless romance, and lush alien landscapes.

Sign up for the Starr Huntress newsletter to get the very latest in releases, promos, giveaways and freebies:
http://eepurl.com/b_NJyr

Facebook: facebook.com/StarrHuntress/
Twitter: @StarrHuntress

CONTENTS

CHAPTER ONE

MYLOMON

MYLOMON HAD TWO OBJECTIVES: FIND THE TRAITOR and eliminate him.

As missions went, it was not the worst assignment his warlord ever gave him. Far from it. Mylomon understood that he made his clan uncomfortable. Mahdfel preferred to confront their enemies directly, challenge them in an honorable manner. Such constricting notions of honor never hindered Mylomon. He followed his warlord's orders. He did his duty. He did the dirty, necessary work that benefited the entire clan. Was it honorable to poison the enemy? Wait for them

1

in the dark and pull them back into the shadows so fast they never felt the knife that sliced their throats? No, but he got shit done. If chest thumping theatrics could corner the traitor, then the warlord would have sent another warrior. But he didn't.

He sent Mylomon.

The *Judgment* had tracked the traitor's signal to the edge of the Terran's system. The battle cruiser monitored the situation but deployed Mylomon for a more nuanced mission on the Terran's lunar base.

Mylomon slipped into the Shackleton Lunar Base unseen. He tracked the traitor's signal to the recreation dome where he discovered some sort of event taking place, a Harvest Festival Ball.

Constructed of a super-dense, transparent material, the top level of the dome was encased in glass. It gave the impression of the room opening directly to space. Terrans and Mahdfel in formal wear filled the room. Music, the constant babble of conversation, colorful decorations, and the aroma of familiar and exotic cuisine threatened to overwhelm his senses.

It also overwhelmed the computer. The program was able to trace the traitor to the recreation dome but it was unable to pinpoint his exact location or distinguish his signal from the thousand other communication units on the arms of every person at the Harvest Festival Ball.

Begrudgingly he admired the traitor's cunning. This mission proved to be more challenging that he anticipated. Good. He hadn't had a real challenge since he moved all the pieces into position to take down the last warlord.

Warlord Omas Nawk had been insane. No one doubted that he had to go. Twisted by an experimental therapy that saved his life, he gained immense strength and stamina. No warrior was able to challenge the warlord in a fair fight.

So Mylomon made it an unfair fight.

He selected who would be the correct warlord to reshape the damaged clan, Omas's brother, Paax. Setting brother against brother was impossible. Paax had left the clan to avoid confronting his deranged brother but Mylomon set in motion the events to motivate Paax to challenge Omas.

Devious? Yes.

Dishonorable? He saved the clan, didn't he? Everything he had done was for the good of the clan.

Like hunting this traitor who leaked security codes

to the Suhlik. Betraying his clan to those alien lizards for what? Mylomon's stomach churned with disgust. What could the Suhlik give a Mahdfel? Nothing. The Suhlik could only take away.

Mylomon's instinct was to hang back in the shadows and observe. The traitor would appear nervous, glancing at the comm unit too often or appear otherwise distracted. The large room was filled with light and sound. There were no shadows. He needed to move about the crowd and blend in as a festival reveler.

He didn't revel. Wasn't in his nature.

He moved through the crowd, trying refrain from stalking, scowling or appearing as a threat. Fortunately, in a crowd of Mahdfel warriors, his size and predatory grace did not set him apart. Unfortunately, he did not have the capacity to appear relaxed, as if he enjoyed the festivities. When someone in the crowd bumped into him, they looked up and their face went pale and they muttered apologies before scurrying away.

Mylomon knew he wasn't conventionally handsome, attractive or even easy to look at, but he wasn't that monstrous, was he?

The festival turned out to be the best place for the traitor to hide from Mylomon.

Unable to move through the crowd without drawing attention to himself, he took up a position on a balcony. With a drink in hand, he slouched against the railing and surveyed the crowd.

On the floor, he spotted Medic Kalen dancing with a dark haired Terran female. This is what the medic did when their warlord sent him away for additional training in Terran biology? Well, he certainly did seem interested in that particular Terran's biology. Mylomon filed away his observation for later use. He never particularly liked or trusted the medic.

A woman brushed by him in a deep purple gown that faded to a bright pink at the hem, arm in arm with a dusky complexion Mahdfel warrior. He paid them no mind, thinking her laugh was too loud.

Then the scent of sunshine and green, growing things hit him.

His head swiveled, tracking the scent back to the woman. She sashayed away with her warrior, continuing to laugh too loud. The movement of the full skirt of her gown was mesmerizing. He could stare at the fabric, and perhaps what was under the fabric, all evening.

His hand rubbed at his chest. Then he paused. He

had no tattoos to tingle at the sight of a mate. He had no markings of clan, family or rank but his skin felt like it was on fire.

For her.

Her blonde hair was pulled on top of her head in a bun. He wanted to free her locks and run his fingers through the blonde waves, gaze into her animated face, open and sweet. This Terran was his mate?

Mylomon shook his head to clear his thoughts. Such sentimentality was beyond him. He never believed he would have a match. The Suhlik had manipulated his genetic material as a child, leaving him an abomination. What were the odds of finding a female genetically compatible with his abnormal genes?

Slim to nonexistent. He gave up the dream of having a mate and a family long ago.

But there she was, the only female in the universe for him, hanging on the arm of another.

Mylomon frowned at his rival, disapproving of the way his formal uniform was unbuttoned at the collar. His hair was a wild, untamed mess. Sloppy. He had a scar on his forehead just below the hairline. Sloppy in battle, too.

He should go over there, press his claim and

challenge the male. He was confident in his skills, both the legitimate skills and the disreputable skills. His prowess would be sure to impress the female.

The itching, burning sensation returned to his chest. Did Terran females enjoy such displays? He only knew one Terran, his warlord's mate, Mercy. She was kind and calm and grew upset at most shows of violence. Her eyes filled with tears and her voice shook in distress when she witnessed her mate being injured in the sparring ring. She said it was *hor-moans* but he did not believe her. Mercy was kind hearted.

Perhaps such a display of his prowess would do more damage than good when it came to impressing his female.

And the blonde female was his, he had no doubt.

He needed to speak to her. Logic told him to walk over to her and say something, anything, but his feet remained rooted in place. She had him as nervous as an untested youth. Foolishness. He should go over there, pull her away from the sloppy warrior and... what, exactly? Throw her over his shoulder and storm away, kidnapping her and abandoning his mission? He didn't know much about Terran females but he was positive they did not enjoy being abducted.

He could ask her name.

Yes, her name. This thought pleased him.

He moved toward her.

She grabbed a slender glass off a tray and downed it quickly, her fair skin blushing with alcohol fueled warmth. With a smile, she playfully jabbed the male on the shoulder.

Mylomon froze. After he asked her name, what then? What if he said the wrong thing? A dozen scenarios played out in his mind, each one ending poorly. No, there was too much at stake for him to casually approach his mate. He needed a plan.

He glanced over the edge of the balcony. In a partially hidden corner, the medic was becoming very familiar with a certain Terran's physiology. Perhaps he discounted the medic too soon. Kalen obviously knew something about females that Mylomon didn't. He would ask for guidance but his relationship with the medic was antagonistic at best. They may be brothers in the same clan but they were not friends.

He should return to the object of his mission. The traitor remained hidden in the crowd. The *Judgment* had intercepted several transmissions, including one with the lunar base's security code. The warlord had decided to remain quiet, to not tip off the traitor that he had been discovered. Now Suhlik forces crowded at the edge of Earth's system, waiting for a signal. Mylomon needed to eliminate the traitor before that signal could be sent.

The female could wait. She was his match. She did not have the scent of a child or another male on her. Eventually she would submit to the screening process and the match would be formalized. This pleased him. Every eligible female was subjected to the screenings. According to the protection treaty his people signed with Earth, childless, single and otherwise healthy females must comply. No exceptions.

Yes, he would wait and she would come to him. Then he would not have to worry about such details as *introductions* and *conversation*. This was a good plan and pleased his assassin instincts. He'd wait for his quarry and prepare all his considerable skill to talk to a girl.

Satisfied, he rubbed at the burning sensation just under the skin of his chest. With preparation, there was no problem he could not overcome.

Alarm klaxons pierced through the music and noise of the crowd, ending the revelry of the festival.

DAISY

CALM, COOL AND COPING. THAT WAS DAISY'S MOTO. So there was absolutely no reason to be fighting back tears. She was giving her friend the send off he deserved. It was far from the end of the world, no matter how much she'd miss Vox.

Pilots cycled in and out of the lunar base often. He'd be back.

"Too bad your Terran blood is too weak for *weskig*," he said. He quickly downed a glass of something pale and green. He gritted his teeth and hissed in satisfaction.

Daisy grabbed a glass. "I will drink your purple butt under the table." She tilted her head back and swallowed the liquor in one gulp, coughing as it burned its way down her throat.

The purple jerk in question gave her an appreciative slap on the back. Dressed in his formal black uniform, Vox hardly looked like the unkempt alien with a dusky heather complexion and wild lavender hair. He looked grown-up.

"Tomorrow is your extraction day," the warrior said.

"We call it a birthday. I was not extracted from my mother." As far as she knew.

"Your mate could be here tonight."

Perched on the balcony, Daisy scanned the crowd. She recognized some of the faces. "Maybe. Maybe not." It didn't matter. Tomorrow she could be matched and her mate would love her and keep her safe, always. She'd never be alone or scared. It did not matter where he was *now* because tomorrow he would be with her.

Daisy had wanted to be matched to a Mahdfel warrior for as long as she could remember. When she was young, hostile aliens, the Suhlik, had invaded Earth. Outgunned and outclassed in every confrontation, Earth needed an ally. The Mahdfel arrived, offering such an alliance. The price? The Mahdfel were once subjugated by the Suhlik and genetically altered. They were altered so they were unable to have female children. The Mahdfel constantly sought out new planets, new alliances, for brides.

And Daisy would to be one of those brides. She knew it in her bones. She just had to wait.

The Mahdfel didn't date or court their women like human men. Potential brides—single, childless and otherwise healthy women—were selected through a genetic matching process. Matches of 98.5 percent compatibility or better were enforced.

An attack during the invasion had left Daisy's sister, Meridan, infertile and exempt from the match. Daisy, however, was hale and hearty.

Daisy could trace the moment her obsession of being matched began back to the attack on Meridan. During the dark days of the invasion, Meridan had been a teen and Daisy maybe eleven, a Suhlik soldier attacked Meridan and their mother. At the refugee camp, an aid worker gave Daisy a cup of salty chicken noodle soup and a package of saltine crackers. She remembered the overwhelming helplessness of the situation as she and her father waited for the medical staff to save her sister. During the long wait, she studied the nurses and doctors. They were not paralyzed by fear. Casualties kept arriving and mortar attacks shook the ground but their work mobilized them. Blood stained the white coats of the doctors and the nurses were just as gory but they were not helpless. They were in control. Daisy wanted to be like them: confident and calm in the face of absolute desperation. That's the moment she decided to be a nurse.

That was also the moment she decided that marrying an alien warrior was the best way to always be safe. So what if it was hero worship? Having her own personal superhero sounded awesome. Daisy remembered clear as day the tall, athletic leaf green alien that defended her sister from the Suhlik soldier and carried her unconscious body to medical care.

Hero worship, justified. Jarron saved Meridan's life. He was unable to save their mother but she was thankful for the gift he gave her that day. A real life superhero. Superman was an alien, too, after all. Just not green.

She worked her way through nursing school and now she worked at the Shackleton Crater Lunar Base, side by side with Earth's alien allies. The alien males weren't interested in dating. Sex, yes, and the odd one-night stand but Daisy wasn't a one-night stand kind of girl. The Mahdfel saw no point in dating if they were going to be matched to a genetically compatible female. Without that compatibility, pregnancy was dangerous for the mother and child, and the Mahdfel wanted a new generation of warriors to carry on the fight against the Suhlik.

Daisy wanted *her* mate. No one else would do. She wanted fireworks and the earth to move. Every birthday she submitted to the test and waited with desperate longing to be matched to her mate. This could be the year, after all.

She spotted her sister's dark hair in the crowd with Kalen. As displeased as Meridan was when Daisy set up their blind-date, they seemed to be getting pretty cozy. Making out, actually.

Vox followed her gaze. He snorted in amusement. "The medic has game."

"Gross," Daisy said, landing an affectionate hit on his shoulder. "That's my sister."

"I see a poker game. I have a powerful need to part fools from their credits."

"I want to dance. Come on, let's dance." She shimmied her hips for emphasis.

"But poker..." The beseeching look was pathetic and effective.

"Fine," Daisy said. "Poker now but when the music is up tempo, we're dancing."

Vox would be gone in the morning. She couldn't wrap her head around not having his ridiculous presence around. At least she would always have Meridan.

"Sounds like a plan to me."

Just as they sat at a table, the alarm klaxons sounded.

CHAPTER TWO

DAISY

KLAXONS SOUNDED, FILLING THE REC DOME WITH A shrill, reverberating alarm. Immediately the alarm on her comm unit sounded. *Suhlik forces incoming*, the message read. *All civilian staff report to designated shelters. Emergency personnel report to their assignments.*

Daisy's assignment was the emergency medical bay. Civilians went to underground shelters, to let the Madhfel and human soldiers do their job of repelling the attack. She would wait in medical, ready to patch them up.

Vox pulled her into a crushing embrace. "I wanted more time," he said. "But I have to go shoot lizards."

"Go," she said, patting him in the center of his chest. "Can you even fly after you've been drinking?"

"I'll need a scrubber."

She'd need one, as well. Once in medical, she'd take a course to remove intoxicants from her system and then change into her nursing scrubs. "Be safe."

Another hug, this one more crushing, more final. "Be safe, sister of my heart."

"Stop it. You're going to make me cry and then all the nurses will make fun of me." She smiled thinly, trying to play off her statement as a joke but they both knew she spoke true.

"I think I need a new scar," he said, gesturing to his chin. "Maybe here. Terran chicks dig scars."

Daisy knew what Vox was doing, making her laugh to avoid tears. They would, most likely, not see each other until the all-clear sounded and then he would be gone to his new deployment. This was the moment for goodbyes. "Get your pretty face out of here and go blow up enemy craft."

"Can't argue with a direct command like that,"

he said, snapping his feet together and giving her a salute.

Then he left, heading down a corridor toward the shuttle bay.

Daisy shivered, rubbing her hands up and down her arms. Medical wasn't far. Above, through the glass dome, small explosions of missiles struck the base's shields. The shielding would hold for several rounds of volleys.

The occupants of the dome moved efficiently and calmly. Even though the Suhlik had not attacked the SCLB in over five years, they were prepared. Civilians practiced heading to the shelters once a month. Emergency personnel, such as herself, were chosen based on their demonstrated ability to stay calm under pressure. The Mahdfel and human soldiers were professionals. No one should panic. Nothing was amiss.

Daisy took the most direct route to medical.

The medical bay wasn't a single location but a cluster of buildings housed in a separate dome, arranged around a green space. Emergency medical was housed in a secondary dome with direct shuttle access to accept the incoming wounded. She could cut through the medical dome with its green lawns, and she normally did on a regular work day, or she could save a few minutes and go the back way through the underground service tunnels.

Daisy clattered down the metal stairs. Above surface, SCLB was functional but not aesthetically pleasing. Human and Mahfel design collided in the most boring fashion. Everything was white or grey. That's what happens when you design by committee: no one is happy but no one can complain. At least SCLB had plenty of green spaces to relieve the monotony of endless grey corridors. Above ground was, at best, functional and inoffensive. Boring.

Below ground was worse. Service tunnels housed pipes and conduits, necessary to maintain the base and life support. Necessary didn't have to mean pretty, it mean bare bones: exposed pipes, plain concrete, and skeleton stairs that always unnerved Daisy. You shouldn't be able to see through the grating on the tread. You just shouldn't.

This particular service tunnel, while warm with steam and illuminated with a sulfurous yellow light from the industrial light fixture, came up right next to the emergency medical bay.

Daisy picked up her dress and ran.

"Female, why are you not in a shelter?"

A loud male voice made her pause. The pronunciation was ever so slightly off. Alien. Some hot-headed warrior intended to shove her in a shelter because she was "someone's female." Happened every drill.

Daisy spun toward the sound of the voice, ready to tell the alien warrior off. Words dried up in her mouth as she took in the male.

Big, that was her first thought. Really big. The shadows gathered to him, even in the sulfurous lighting. His deep aubergine complexion was the perfect shade to blend into the dark. Horns curled aggressively from his forehead, coming to a wickedly sharp point. Daisy had the overwhelming urge to run a finger along those horns and test their sensitivity. Theoretically she knew the horns were sensitive but touching a male's horns was an intimate activity. She never touched any male's horns, not even Vox's, but she *needed* to touch his.

He strode toward her, long legs eating up the distance between them.

He wasn't handsome, not by any stretch of the imagination. His features were far too sharp. Lips too thin. Chin too hard. Stars, he was compelling. He practically radiated danger and dominance.

She wanted to run her hands over him, explore the broad splendor of his chest, ripples of his abs and strength of his thighs. She just wanted to lick him all over like he was giant purple lollipop.

Stars, that sounded like a good idea.

Excitement fluttered in her chest. Working side by side with alien males for more than two years and not a single one had ever turned her head. Well... she enjoyed the eye candy but none had ever made her weak in the knees. Literally weak in the knees. She needed to sit.

Daisy leaned a shoulder against the wall.

"Are you injured, female?"

"No, I'm fine," Daisy said.

The male came forward and reached for her. Daisy evaded. "Listen," she said, "I need to get to emergency medical."

"You are injured." His eyes narrowed as if he visually tried to confirm her injuries.

"I'm not injured. I need to report to my station. You know, to do my job." Speaking of which, why wasn't this warrior at his station?

"You should be in a shelter with the other Terrans."

Not this garbage again. "Look, I'm a combat nurse.

See." She thrust her wrist comm toward him. "That's my assignment. Let me do my job."

His hand wrapped around her wrist, warm and surprisingly soft. Shouldn't a warrior have hardened, calloused hands? And why, oh why, did she need to have his warm hands all over her. His thumb brushed against the tender skin of her inner wrist. His eyes held hers, dark and turbulent. "You are too precious to be risked. Allow me to bring you to a shelter."

For a moment, she was tempted. Going with him seemed like a good idea. A *fun* idea. And she'd been drinking at the Harvest Festival Ball. She was hardly fit for duty. Her supervisor would understand if she was too incapacitated to make it to emergency medical.

She blinked to clear her head. No. She was a professional, not a giggling school girl ready to go make out with the hot guy while the base was under attack. Plus, if they lingered too long, they risked being sealed into the tunnels.

She yanked her hand away. "No. I need to report to my station."

He moved to grab her arm. Asking nicely was over, apparently.

Daisy darted away, running up the stairs. The

ground shuddered. She clung to the railing but kept climbing. The shielding was down. How were the shields down so quickly? Those things could take a pounding for hours, or so the orientation video had claimed.

The stairs spilled into a nondescript corridor. Grey, of course. Another ground shake. For the first time, Daisy regretted her heels. Keeping her footing in the ridiculous shoes was a challenge she did not need at the moment.

She glanced at the ceiling. It appeared stable. Rationally she knew the domes covering the base were highly resistant to direct hits and the base had fail safes to protect against a breach. Corridors would seal themselves off, isolating the rip or tear, if such an unlikely thing were to happen.

She took a deep breath. Calm. Cool. Collected. She chanted her mantra. The base was safe. Safer than anything on Earth. Safer than the little wooden house her family had lived in during the initial Suhlik invasion. Safer than the bombed out church basement they had squatted in. There was no safer place to be than on the moon.

She rounded the corner. Not much farther now.

The dark warrior continued to chase her. He could easily run her down, tackle her, and carry her kicking and screaming into a shelter. He didn't want her frightened, she reasoned, so he followed at a distance. It didn't matter. She was nearly there. Once in emergency medical, he wouldn't be able to remove her.

One more set of doors and she'd be there. The doors slide open as Daisy approached, only to reveal a corridor full of Suhlik. Tall, gorgeous, deadly Suhlik.

What. The. Hell.

Daisy skidded to a stop. Collectively, their golden, ethereally beautiful faces turned toward her. Their eyes were so large, so intriguing. No being had the right to be that pretty. Or that dangerous. She wanted to lay down at their feet, let them tear out her throat with their two rows of teeth.

The dark warrior shoved Daisy behind him. He growled at the Suhlik warriors. They responded in kind. This made no sense. The Suhlik should not be here, in Earth space or on the moon. Too many sophisticated defense systems were in place to allow a raiding party to just casually stroll into the lunar base. And why hadn't the shields held?

"What are those lizards doing here?"

"Female," the Mahdfel warned.

Yeah, yeah. She didn't like the derogatory word either but if you couldn't use it when you were moments away from being gutted by a beautiful space lizard, when could you?

The Suhlik hissed. Her implanted chip was slow to translate but she didn't need it to know it meant nothing good. Then the Suhlik moved as one and rushed toward them.

Her dark warrior pulled her toward him. Then he did the unexpected. They moved toward the wall.

Into the wall.

Through the wall.

The world went fuzzy at the edges—just like when she used a teleporter and was being scattered to the stars. Only this time, she went sideways through a wall instead of across space. Her stomach decided that now was the time for somersaults and then her head hit something solid. Hard.

Darkness.

MYLOMON

Events failed to comply with his plan.

He followed his mate to insure her safety—no other reason. When the alarm first sounded, he hesitated, torn between assuring his mate's safety and continuing to track the traitor. His hesitation caused the mission to fail and allowed the traitor to slip away in the chaos. He spoke to his mate—unscripted, unprepared and against the plan. His only consolation was that her body responded to his: elevated heart rate, raised body temperature, dilated pupils, tightening nipples. She even licked her lips as her hungry gaze admired his form. Running through the bowels of the base might explain the heart rate and body temperature but not the lip licking. The lip licking was all for him.

Then she ran head first into a cluster of Suhlik warriors.

Suhlik. The idea of that filth daring to set foot on a Mahdfel controlled base enraged him on many levels. He cursed inferior Terran designs, the traitor that lowered the shields, and the lack of hellstone in the structure of the base. No hellstone? What were the

Terrans thinking? Hellstone's unique chemical property prevented teleportation.

The Terrans utilized teleportation technology every day. They knew the Suhlik had the same tech. Why had they failed to add hellstone to the domes, walls and very foundation of the base?

Terrans never listened. They blathered on about budgets and probability and look where it got them: a moon base filled with Suhlik.

His female failed to listen to him, as well. If she had, she would have been safely below ground in a shelter with the rest of the Terran civilians. No. Why should one single thing go smoothly? Better to continue the string of calamity, which he did with a less-than-perfect teleport. Faced with charging Suhlik, his first instinct was to greet his opponent with a smile in battle, but he had to think of his mate. He had to protect her. Terrans were soft skinned and fragile. Terran females were particularly small. Delicate. He could not allow his delicate Terran female to be injured, so he wrapped his arms around her and shifted through the wall.

Teleporting a second person required perfect clarity and concentration. He had neither. The shift was flawed and she injured her head. He injured her with his sloppiness. Unacceptable.

Overhead lighting flickered on and he surveyed their new environment. They were in some kind of a room. Terran sized furniture cluttered the space, giving the room the tedious look of an administrator's office. The thin door was not designed to withstand enemy fire. This was an unacceptable location. His unconscious mate would not be safe here.

He would find an acceptable location and guard her until she woke.

He lifted his mate and slung her across his shoulders. She weighed next to nothing. A light floral scent emanated from her golden hair. He wanted to bury his nose in it and breath it in but now was not the time. Suhlik were infiltrating the base. A traitor had lowered the shields and allowed them in. His mate was injured. No, it was definitely not a good time to contemplate flowers and his female's delicious scent.

Mylomon jogged into the hall. His mate wanted to go to the medical bay. He would bring her there. Several warriors would guard the medical facility. She would be safe and a medic could look at her head.

The door at the end of the corridor would not

open. Safety protocols had put barricades in place to isolate the intruders. He could teleport through the barrier, bringing his mate along but he was reluctant. He could not risk losing his concentration and injuring his mate again. He would find another way.

Mylomon backtracked and took a different path. This corridor branched into several but lead him away from the medical facilities. The fire of plasma rifles sounded in the distance. The ground shook from missile strikes but the dome continued to hold. Lights flickered but the dome still held. He was glad his mate remained unconscious. She did not have to worry about sudden atmospheric loss.

He rounded another corner, displeased with the growing distance between him and his target location. He had memorized the layout of the base but the rerouting made it difficult to get his bearings. All he knew was where he was *not*.

The corridor emptied out into a larger common space. Warriors clashed with Suhlik, as they should. His brothers fought well, defending their homes and their own mates. It was an impressive sight, part of him yearned to join the fray, but it was not the way forward.

Mylomon moved to retrace his steps. A Suhlik male blocked his exit. Three more joined their comrade.

He tilted his head to one side. Only four. He calculated the odds. He was faster and more vicious, just as the Suhlik had made him. But his mate's life depended on him. He could not leave her unguarded, not for a single moment.

Footsteps. More Suhlik approached. Options dwindling, Mylomon pulled his mate down from his shoulders and held her to his chest. The more of her that touched him, the easier the teleport.

The Suhlik closest to him raised a weapon. The plasma rifled hummed as it prepared a charge.

Mylomon sank through the floor, into the unknown, clutching his mate.

CHAPTER THREE

DAISY

A THUMPING HEADACHE WOKE HER. SHE WAS ON her back on a cold, hard surface. The floor, her sluggish brain supplied. If the needling pain behind her eyes had been a tad less excruciating, she might be upset to find herself on the floor.

Daisy rolled to her side and pushed herself off the floor. Memories filtered in. The ball. She drank but not excessively, not near enough to warrant this level of headache. Alarms. Suhlik. Right. The base was under attack. Then there was that obnoxious warrior who insisted she go to a shelter when she needed to report to the emergency medical bay. What a jerk.

First, assess the situation.

She was in the dark. On a floor. Her eyes gradually adjusted. Emergency lighting provided the barest of illumination: a stripe on the floor leading to a door and dim recessed lighting that cast just enough light to not run into furniture. Speaking of furniture, there was a table in the center of the room that reminded her of a surgery platform. The light gleamed off metal panels that were built into the wall, each panel a perfect square. She recognized the room as the auxiliary morgue, to be used in the event of catastrophic casualties from an attack or if a disease outbreak swamped the medical bay. This was not an approved shelter. No one came here.

She shivered from the cold. No one was meant to shelter here. Life support was minimal and the temperature remained cold, to preserve the... She swallowed, refusing to finish the thought. Calm, cool and coping, she repeated in her head. She was above a freak out. She was a nurse with combat experience. She'd been soaked in the blood of wounded human soldiers and alien warriors.

An unused, empty morgue would not frighten her.

She listened. No sounds. No alarms. No voices. Not even another person breathing, just the regular white noise of the base—generators, ventilation system— that she normally filtered into the background. She was alone in the dark.

"You are awake," an unfamiliar voice in the dark said.

Daisy yelped in surprise, her heart pounding. "What the hell is going on? Who are you? Where am I?" Her words came out in a jumble. Not the cool, calm demeanor she wanted to project. Taking a deep breath, she faced the direction of the voice and tried again. "Can you tell me what's happening and why my head is pounding like a jackhammer?"

A Mahdfel male leaned forward.

Daisy scrambled backwards.

Faint lighting illuminated his dark purple complexion, casting half his face into shadow. Every line on his face was harsh and cruel. His horns curled out aggressively from his forehead. His eyes gleamed with... expectation? It was hard to read his face in the poor lighting. She recognized him as the warrior who prevented her from reporting to her post.

He frowned at the way she flinched backwards. He squatted on his heels, as if trying to make his bulk smaller and less threatening.

Daisy took a deep, calming breath. She didn't know he was cruel. That was fear talking, not reason. "Sorry, you surprised me."

He grunted.

"Big talker, huh?"

"What is there to discuss? I surprised you. That was not my intention but it happened."

Understatement of the year. Something half-remembered tickled at her. "Did you— Did you go through a wall?"

He was slow to answer, which lead Daisy to think yes. Yes he did smash through a wall like the Hulk or the Kool-Aid Man. Her head certainly felt like they smashed through a wall. She rubbed her forehead, letting her cold hand sooth her aching head. "I think I hit my head when you knocked down that wall. Where are we?"

"We are safe."

"Okay, let's try again," Daisy said. "I know this is the auxiliary morgue. Why are we here?"

"You were in danger."

"I wasn't in danger. I was *trying* to get to my post so I could do my job."

"The Suhlik breached the base."

"Which is why I need to be at my post in the emergency medical bay!" She threw her hands up in frustration.

"The way was blocked. You could not arrive safely."

"So you stuffed me in here?"

Another grunt. Fantastic.

"Shouldn't you be out there fighting, warrior?"

"My duty is to protect you, female."

Daisy pushed herself off the floor, stumbling on the hem of the dress, and made her way to the door. Most rooms in the base locked down automatically when the alarms sounded. Civilians and staff had a few minutes to get to their assigned shelters or their stations. After ten minutes, the doors locked to contain civilians in the shelter until the threat passed. If someone remain in their quarters or other location, they were also locked down to prevent civilians wandering the corridors in the middle of a firefight. Only a few select areas of the base did not go into lockdown. The morgue might be one of them.

Daisy placed her hand against the control panel.

It remained unresponsive. She punched in a code. No joy. She slammed her hand against the control panel, then pounded on the door. Finally, she kicked it.

"Female, cease or you will injure yourself."

She ignored him and spoke into her comm unit.

"Please keep this channel free for emergency use. Try your request later."

"I am emergency personnel. A big purple—" Daisy bit her tongue. Her instinct was to say *idiot* but the big purple idiot in question was scary looking, so it was better not to antagonize. "I'm stuck in the aux morgue."

"Please keep this channel free for emergency use. Try your request later."

Well, that was garbage.

She spun toward him. "Open it."

"No."

"Use your clearance and open the door." A warrior could override the locks, as a safety precaution.

"I only arrived this day and do not have a security clearance yet."

Fan-fucking-tastic. Why would he have a security clearance? "Come on. Use all that muscle and knock down the door, then."

"I will not." He rose to his feet, his full height looming above her. Stars, he was big. Her head came to his mid-chest, right at his pecs. For a moment she wondered how hard those pecs would feel under her hands. Like stone. Everywhere. Most Mahdfel warriors were muscular and beefy. Perfect masculine specimens didn't turn her head anymore but this male... He was different. Bigger, like they fed him steroids. Part of her wanted to take off that stiff, formal uniform and explore all those muscles. That same part wasn't too upset about being stuck in a room with him. Alone. For who knows how long.

She blinked, focusing on her frustration at the situation and not the frustration stirring between her thighs. "Then what's the point of you!"

He leaned down, top lip pulled back in a sneer. "That door is infused with nanocarbon. I cannot simple knock it down. Even if I could get past that barrier, the base is swarming with Suhlik. You have no armor. No weapon. They will eviscerate you."

Daisy refused to flinch at his words. She held his gaze. "I'd be careful. Emergency medical is not far."

"No." He folded his arms over his chest. "Female, this discussion is over."

Daisy inspected the room, hands rubbing her bare arms. Intentionally kept cold, the space was not designed to accommodate a person sitting and hanging out, waiting for the all-clear. She opened the storage drawers along the wall. All empty. No cabinets. No cloth or blanket. Not even a chair, just a cold metal table in the center of the room.

"You are cold," the male said.

"Yes. The temperature is kept low in here for... storage."

He shrugged off his jacket, revealing his bare chest, and handed it to her. She accepted it after a moment's hesitation. She didn't want any help from him but she didn't want to freeze, either. The jacket was stiff and scratchy but also warm.

He nodded with satisfaction.

Daisy paced the length of the room. She should ask his name. That would be the polite thing to do. They could be in there for hours, maybe even a day. She couldn't keep calling him "warrior". But if she asked for his name, then he'd ask for hers and then what would she say? "Sorry, Charlie. That information is classified."

Actually, that might be really satisfying. Rude, yes, but satisfying.

"You should rest, female," he said.

Daisy clenched her teeth, fighting back a scream. *Female*. Yes, all the alien males used that term but when *he* said it, the term made her blood pressure sky rocket.

Actually, if he had a name he might stop calling her female.

"That's Nurse Vargas to you, bub."

"You should rest."

"On what, the cold floor? The cold metal table?" Not going to happen.

"Your shoes are unstable and the way you walk indicates they pinch your toes."

"You are not criticizing my shoes right now, are you? Because I don't know if I can stay polite but need I remind you that I'm only stuck in here because of you." The shoes did hurt her feet but she refused to admit that to him.

"I removed you from danger and protected you."

"You blocked me from doing my job!"

He sat cross legged on the floor and patted his lap. "I will keep you warm, Nurse Vargas."

"You have got to be kidding me."

"Then continue to pace and shiver. Let your pride impede your wellbeing."

Daisy narrowed her eyes at him. "This isn't about my pride."

He patted his lap again.

"Fine," she said at length. "But no touching or coping a feel, got it? This is just about warmth."

He nodded. "As you say, female."

MYLOMON

HIS MATE WAS DISPLEASED WITH HIM. THEY HAD ONLY just met and already he had said and done the wrong thing.

She was upset that he'd prevented her from going to her post, but the Suhlik surrounded them. He'd had no choice. If he'd stepped aside as she wished, she would have been injured or worse. And he would be alone again. Perhaps there was another match for him but most likely not. Nurse Vargas was a miracle, made just for him.

No, he was right to do as he did. Better to have a mate angry and alive with him than pleased and deceased.

When she acquiesced and agreed to sit in his lap, strictly for warmth, his heart seized with joy. If he could not please his mate with his actions, perhaps his physical presence would suffice. He kept his arms loose around her as she settled in. Her back was rigid, shoulders stiff. After a few minutes, she relaxed and pressed her back to his chest.

He resisted the urge to lean down and sniff her hair, breathing in the floral scent of her shampoo.

"How long have we been in here?"

"Several hours, female."

She made a disgruntled noise. "I wish you wouldn't call me that."

"Female?"

"Yes. I have a name, you know."

It took all of his will to resist stroking her hair and pressing a kiss to her temple. He was not worthy to utter her name. He would not say it until she graced him with a smile.

"Fine, be that way," she said with a yawn. She pulled the jacket tighter around her.

It might be some time.

"You should sleep," he said.

"No chance, bub. I don't trust you and I'm certainly not taking a nap in your lap."

He smirked at her rhyme. "You will remain unharmed."

"Wow, that doesn't sound menacing at all."

Mylomon frowned. His errors kept mounting. She found him threatening. Frightening. Perhaps it was best she did not learn his name. With the poor lighting, she would be unable to get a good look at him. By the time they were matched, her memories of this night would be fuzzy. His next attempt to win the affection of his mate would be successful.

Yes, time is what he needed. Time to plan. Time to research her and learn her likes and dislikes. Time to prepare his stark quarters aboard the *Judgment* to better accommodate a soft Terran female.

The light from her wrist comm unit illuminated her face. "Stupid data," she muttered. "No network, no onboard memory. But why would I need memory on this thing when the network is always on?"

"What are you doing?"

"I want to watch a movie or read a book or something but the network is in emergency mode. No streaming. No downloading from my library. This cheap government model doesn't have onboard storage." Another yawn.

"You should sleep."

She twisted around to face him. "I told you, no. I don't trust you or even know your name."

Intriguingly soft in the most appealing places, her ass had just the right amount of substance. He enjoyed the way it felt on his lap. An iron clad will kept his cock from standing at attention and announcing just how much he enjoyed her softness.

He had nothing if not control. He could give her a name, to ease her worry at being trapped with a stranger. He could give her that peace of mind. Yes, he liked the notion.

"Mylomon," he said.

She repeated his name, a smile pulling at the corner of her soft lips. Satisfied they had been properly introduced, she snuggled against his chest. "That wasn't too hard, was it, Mylo?"

He rumbled with pleasure.

CHAPTER FOUR

DΛISY

THE ALL-CLEAR ON HER COMM UNIT BEEPED. HER eyes were extraordinarily heavy and her neck stiff. She wasn't in her bed. A moment of fuzzy recollection and then she knew exactly where she spent the night: trapped in the auxiliary morgue with Mylomon.

The warrior had insisted she sleep curled in his lap like he was a piece of furniture. For warmth, of course. No other reason. The night had been... oddly pleasant. He kept his hands to himself and despite being solid muscle, she fit comfortably against him.

Incoming messages flooded her comm unit. The first dozen were security alerts, then her supervisor trying to locate her and then finally from Vox.

Daisy jumped off the floor and out of Mylomon's lap. "I have to get to the medical bay." Her sister had been injured during the attack. Badly.

The door opened automatically as Daisy approached it. She ran down the corridor and up the service stairwell. Scorch marks from laser rifles decorated the walls. She ignored the obvious signs of conflict in the dome as she raced toward medical. Meridan filled her thoughts. Vox kept the message brief. "Meridan hurt. Medical. Now." He sent several other updates but Daisy was too concerned about getting to her sister's side to stop and read them.

Emergency medical hummed with activity, patching up plenty of soldiers and a few civilians. Daisy headed straight for the front desk. The woman behind the counter recognized Daisy and pointed down a corridor toward Critical Care.

Her mind went blank. All Daisy heard was the thumping of her heart. She was eleven years old all over again, rushing to the medical tent in the refugee camp, searching for her mother and sister. Her father's hand gripping hers tight enough to bruise. She was helpless then. There was little she could do now.

Vox found her and pulled her into an embrace. Then he brought her into the room with the regeneration tanks. He sat her down in a chair in front of Meridan, who floated naked in a vat of green goo. Her dark hair fanned out like a mermaid. Eyes closed, unconscious, Meridan was oblivious to the tubes attached to every orifice and the vicious red marks where her flesh had been sliced open. Surgical glue and plastic lattice held her together.

Daisy pressed the palm of her hand to the tank. "What happened?"

"She was accosted by a Suhlik patrol."

"But why wasn't she in the shelter?" Meridan should have been in a civilian shelter.

"I do not know. She sent a distress signal that the Suhlik had breached the base."

Daisy nodded, absently. "They cornered me, too."

Vox placed a hand on her shoulder. "Are you well?"

"I'm fine."

He spun her to face him. "Are you well?"

Tears filled her eyes and she shook her head. "No,"

she said in a small voice. "Why is she in a regen tank? Who authorized it?"

"I did." Medic Kalen entered the room and inspected the tank's readings.

"That's not cleared for human use," Daisy said. She wiped away the moisture clinging to her lashes. She refused to be helpless now. Meridan needed her and she had exactly the right skills to help. She wasn't that useless little girl caught in the invasion. Not anymore.

"Her injuries were too extensive." He rattled off an impossible list: punctured lung, fractured ribs, arms, multiple lacerations, and extreme blood loss. Even her kidneys were injured. "This is the best course of treatment."

Daisy took a closer look at the alien medic. His face was haggard and drawn, like he had run all night on nothing but adrenaline. "When did you rest?"

"I can't. Not yet."

Daisy took the tablet from him. "You have to rest. You won't do Merri any good if you burn yourself out."

He nodded but his eyes did not leave Meridan's floating figure in the tank. "I don't want her to be alone."

He cared for Meridan. The realization surprised Daisy. Even though she'd set them up on a date for the ball—was it only last night? —she believed their mutual attraction was superficial. Meridan and Kalen had been flirting terribly for the last two weeks. The genuine concern, the deep despair at her injuries, told her that Meridan was more than a casual flirtation for the alien physician.

"I'll sit with her," Daisy said. "She won't be alone. You rest. Then we can trade places."

Daisy sat for several hours in an uncomfortable chair. Vox brought her a dry sandwich and a lukewarm coffee. He sat beside her, holding her hand. Eventually the shuttle bay called him away for his deployment. At some point Kalen returned, still tired but marginally less haggard. He spoke via the view screen to a Mahdfel male with one horn. His warlord, she supposed. She paid him no attention. The only thing that mattered was the information streaming to her tablet from the regen tank. All levels were within acceptable parameters. She refreshed. All levels continued to be within acceptable parameters.

At some point a warrior arrived to escort her to the testing facility. It was her birthday, after all. Time to be matched.

Daisy barely noticed the nurse drawing blood. She pressed her thumb to the tablet when prompted. She nodded as the nurse spoke but nothing got through the barrier of worry and dread filling her head.

"Daisy? Did you hear me?"

"What? Yes. No. I mean, can you repeat yourself." She blinked rapidly, forcing herself to pay attention.

"You have a match."

"No, you're wrong. I never have a match."

"You do have a match," the nurse repeated.

How could that be? Merri was stuck in a tank that might or might not repair her. She couldn't be matched and whisked away. "My sister needs me. I can't leave."

"Well, good news there," the nurse said, consulting her tablet. "Your match is actually on SCLB."

"Oh." So her match had been here all along. Did she know him? Had they met? Smiled at each other in passing? Then the practical logistics of a match percolated in. "I have so many clothes to pack. Why did I buy so much useless stuff?"

A dark figure entered the room. Daisy recognized the dark warrior. Mylomon. Shirtless. Of course. She couldn't help but roll her eyes. So many Mahdfel males preened about without their shirts on. Desensitized to all the man-flesh on display, something about the way the light hit his sculpted pecs made her lick her lips. Exhaustion and attraction was a strange mix.

He cocked an eyebrow at her.

"You want your jacket back. Sorry, I got distracted." She shrugged it off.

"You may keep it, mate," he said.

No way.

No freaking way.

This guy? The guy that kept her from doing her job? That kept her from her sister's side?

"You do know each other. Fantastic," the nurse said brightly. She held up the tablet for Daisy's thumbprint. "Just indicate here and here. I know you know all the regulations. We're all done. Congratulations."

MYLOMON

HE NEEDED TO ADJUST HIS PLAN. AGAIN. RATHER THAN having a month or even a year to prepare, the time frame shifted forward. A lot forward. Unprepared and without notice, he had his mate.

He now knew her full name: Daisy Vargas. He rolled her name around on his tongue, enjoying the shape of her name.

She was unhappy to learn of their match. Perhaps he should have been bold last night and boasted of his achievements and his rank. He was second in command in his clan and answered only to the warlord. He had bested many enemies in battle.

Perhaps. Mylomon rubbed absently at his chest. He did not believe that his mate was the type of female such deeds impressed. She worked alongside many valiant and decorated warriors. Rank and a few scars would not turn her head. And he wanted to impress her, prove himself a worthy mate.

Prepared to recite his achievements and all that recommended him as a worthy, he strode into the testing facility.

"Oh, no. Not going to happen," she said, stopping his plan before it began.

"Female, we are matched."

"But you? Seriously?"

What was wrong with him? Doubt stabbed at him. He knew his appearance was not as pleasing to Terran females as other members of his clan. There was little he could do about that though.

"Female, we will return to my clan. Prepare yourself."

Her face screwed up with anger. "Female? Are we back to that again? My name is Daisy."

He gave her a long look, sweeping up from her feet to her scowling face. She still wore the purple gown and his jacket. Oversized on her, like a child playing dress up, she appeared tired. Circles hung under her eyes. Her hair, so lovely the night before, was in disarray. Tired and probably hungry, it was clear she hadn't cared for herself since running away from him that morning. Was he that abhorrent in her eyes?

"You are tired. You should rest and I will make preparations." There. He was a male who knew to give the care a delicate Terran female required.

"No." She took a step toward him, chin lifted definitely.

"Female," he growled in frustration.

"You don't get to dictate where I go and what I do." Another step forward. Now a finger poked him in the chest. If any other Terran had dared to defy him in such a manner, he'd have broken their finger. When Daisy did it, he grumbled in displeasure.

"I am your mate. The match decided."

"Not last night, I wasn't."

"You were in danger." Did she not understand that? The Suhlik had her surrounded. There was no easy escape from that situation.

"You stopped me from doing my job! And while I was stuck with you, my sister was attacked. She needed me and I was trapped in a room *with you*." Another jab. Despite her obvious anger, the jab was not forceful enough to cause him concern.

"Do not do that again. You will injure yourself."

"Do what?" She cocked her head to one side. "This?" Another jab, hard and determined.

He nearly grinned. She had fire in her blood.

He bent down, face close to hers. "That."

Her dark eyes went wide and she took a step back. "I'm not going anywhere until my sister is out of that regen tank."

"As you say."

Confusion flashed across her expressive face. In the poor lighting last night, he'd missed that detail.

His mate had an expressive face that betrayed her thoughts. "Just like that?"

"You worry for your kin. You will be unhappy if we leave before you are satisfied of her recovery. There is no benefit in an unhappy mate."

That determined set to her chin again. "As long as it *benefits* you," she said.

Mylomon was at a complete loss to understand how his proclamation displeased her. "You need to rest. And eat."

"Right, right," Daisy muttered. "An exhausted mate is of no benefit to you."

He escorted her to her modest quarters.

"This is me," she said, unlocking the door with the palm of her hand.

He moved to follow her inside.

"What are you doing?"

"You are my mate," he said, to make it obvious to her. He would not leave her unprotected, not after the Suhlik had infiltrated the moon base.

"You think that means you're moving in?" She folded her arms over her chest, blocking the door.

Apparently he needed to make it more plain to his mate. "It is my duty to protect you, female. The Suhlik were here, inside the base's shields. They can return. I will not leave your side until I am satisfied that the base is secure."

"And you're in charge of SCLB's security now?"

He growled in frustration. If only she knew of the mission that brought him to this damnable base. "I am in charge of your security."

She sighed dramatically but stepped to the side. "Fine. No funny business. I'm not in the mood."

He nodded. He would refrain from jovial behavior and remain serious in her presence.

The interior was a riot of colors and textiles. This female obvious had not met a throw blanket or pillow that she did not like. Every conceivable surface was covered with the items. He followed her into the bedroom. She pushed him out and closed the door.

He settled down on the overly-plush sofa, sinking into the cushions. The distant sounds of a shower filtered into the cramped common area. He would take this opportunity to update his warlord. Then procure sustenance for his mate. She would be hungry. Being angry at him probably worked up an appetite.

DΛISY

Voices drifted in from the common room. Fresh out of the shower and wrapped in nothing but a towel, Daisy paused to listen. Muffled, the voices were indistinct but she recognized the low rumble of Mylomon's voice. He spoke to another male. Curiosity got the better of her and she crept to the door to eavesdrop. Rude? Yes, but he was in her apartment. It'd be irresponsible for her not to listen.

She pressed an ear to the door, listening carefully.

"The traitor has left the base," a low voice said. Mylomon, she recognized.

A traitor. That explained how the Suhlik had been able to breach SCLB's defenses so quickly. Someone had either lowered the shield or gave the Suhlik the access codes.

"The *Judgment* has been busy chasing Suhlik out of the system. I don't have time to track down all your odds and ends," an unknown male said.

"I understand, Sir." He must be speaking with his warlord.

"But I did. I captured a transmission, which points

us toward a research facility on a dead planet."

"Is that what the Suhlik wanted here?"

"What do they always want?"

No reply.

"One of the traitors is Terran," the warlord said.

A chill went down Daisy's spine. The Suhlik had not attacked Earth in a decade and had not attacked in the system for several years, until last night. Now the aliens claimed a human had betrayed their own kind.

She didn't follow politics and had no interest in hot topic talk shows. People had been protesting the Protection Treaty for fourteen years, even though Earth had little choice, and people continued to protest. They didn't approve of Earth women being married off to alien men. Not because it took away the autonomy of the woman. Nope. They just didn't want the species to mix. Usually that's when Daisy tuned it out. Maybe she should had paid more attention. Maybe people were getting tired of the genetic matches and wanted to end the treaty. But then why invite the Suhlik to attack the SCLB? That made no sense. The attack would only reinforce Earth's need for the Mahdfel's protection.

"Shall I eliminate the Terran traitor?" Mylomon asked.

"Not necessary. The council wishes us to continue to monitor the situation."

"Understood."

"How long until you return to us?"

"There's been a complication, sir."

"I heard." The warlord chuckled. "And when did you have time to find a mate while you were failing to track our traitor?"

"The match is beyond even my control." Mylomon didn't sound happy. "My mate's sister was injured in the attack. She insists we stay until her sister is recovered."

"Hmm. My head medic has also found a reason to remain on the base."

"Injuries were high."

"Casualties?"

"None."

Daisy breathed out a sigh of relief. No casualties.

"And how is your mate, sir?" Mylomon asked. The conversation shifted from a debriefing to casual conversation.

"She has the pregnancy brain. I am told it is normal but I do not approve."

"I want to talk to Mylomon," a woman said.

"Warlord's female," Mylomon said, voice formal. An unexpected surge of jealousy swept over her. Her husband was talking to another woman. The feeling was crazy. Inexplicable. She barely knew Mylo and certainly could not expect him to never speak to another woman, but the possessive jealousy remained.

"Is it true your mate has a medical background?"

"She is a nurse," Mylomon said.

"Where is she? I'd like to speak with her."

"She is resting."

"Oh really?" The presumptive tone made Daisy blush.

"Her sister was injured in the attack. She is exhausted."

"She doesn't like you, does she?" The pure glee in the woman's tone angered Daisy. Why did the warlord's female—dammit, wife, she corrected her thought— take such joy in Daisy not liking Mylo? It made her want to come to Mylo's defense, to stride out there and announced that she did not dislike her husband.

Daisy gasped, realizing it was true. She didn't dislike Mylomon. She might even like him a little bit.

The alien male in question turned toward her door and frowned.

The woman continued, "Be sure to blow up her house and then stab her. That always wins over the chicks."

The warlord murmured something not picked up on the audio feed.

"I will not let it go," the woman said. "I don't care whose orders it was. He stabbed me. I'm allowed to have a grudge. And you're supposed to entertain the whimsies of a pregnant women, Paax."

"Stabbing my second is not a whimsy."

"You may stab me if it will appease your sense of justice," Mylomon said.

What kind of crazy clan had she gotten herself hitched to?

"You will not," the warlord commanded.

"Fine," the woman said. "Bring me chocolate. The stuff out of the reconstructor is waxy. And good chocolate, too. Ask your wife. She'll know."

Mylomon said nothing. Daisy could only assume he nodded.

"The *Judgment* will continue its pursuit of the Suh-lik out of this system. When your mate's sister is re-covered, you will return."

"Understood, sir."

The conversation terminated. Footsteps gave her little warning to scramble back from the door and jump into bed and pretend to be asleep. The door opened and Mylomon towered above her, dark and menacing.

"You do not have to crouch at doors, female," he said. "I cannot share details of my missions with you but I will not hide it from you."

"There's a traitor on the base?"

"A detail I cannot share."

"That's why you were here during the attack."

He nodded.

Daisy sat on the edge of her bed. New information from the day swirled inside her mind, it was a lot to process. Almost too much. "Thank you," she said, "for waiting until Merri is recovered."

He nodded and left the room.

Daisy collapsed backwards onto the bed and chuck-led, more out of nerves than amusement. Her husband was such a big talker.

CHAPTER FIVE

MYLOMON

DAYS BLED TOGETHER. MYLOMON WAS NO CLOSER to locating the traitor than he had been the night of the attack. All signs indicated that the traitor had left the base the next day, hidden in a deployment.

His mate's sister continued to improve each day. The medical jargon Daisy used to communicate with Kalen flew above his head but the tension slowly vanished from their bodies. The visible scars faded from Meridan. Her body responded to the treatment. This pleased his mate, which pleased him. Then the unexpected occurred. The regeneration tank treated not only the life threatening trauma but the older injuries as well. New scars vanished. So did the old.

As her sister improved, Daisy's mood soured.

His mate argued with a technician when he arrived.

"I don't care. I won't give consent to have her tested."

"The test is mandatory for every eligible woman," the technician said.

"You need Merri to be awake to give consent, or family. That's me. And I'm telling you to get stuffed." Daisy crossed her arms over her chest in a move that signaled the end of that discussion. The technician stormed away with threats of contacting a supervisor.

"What is wrong, female?" Mylomon asked.

His mate turned her head slightly to acknowledge his presence then returned her attention to the tablet. "Nothing's wrong."

"You do not smile."

She sighed. "Just because I'm not smiling doesn't mean something's wrong. And why can't you wear a damn shirt!"

Ah, now she was upset and deflecting. He heard about this technique of Terran females. If she insisted he display his observational skills, he would. "So you say. Your sister continues to improve but your disposition has shifted from worry to dread. You eat and you sleep but you do not take sustenance or rest. You stare at the tablet, upset at what that data tells you. For every problem removed from the list, you frown, this is counter to the relief one would expect. So tell me truly, female, what is wrong, and do not say it is a shirt."

"It's Merri's birthday today," Daisy said. Mylomon cocked his head to one side, waiting for her to explain. "She has a medical exemption from being matched, you know. Well, had. She had been infertile because of an old injury but the regen tank fixed it. I'm not sure if Merri's going to be happy or peeved."

"She will be pleased."

Daisy shook her head. "You don't know her like I do." She paused, pressing her palm to the glass of the tank. "She's always taken care of me. Of others. And one day soon, she's going to wake up, you'll take me away and I'll never see her again." Her voice made a strangled noise. Tears. Her breath gasped and hitched in her throat. His mate cried.

He approached her, unsure of what to do but needing to be near. Daisy surprised him by throwing her arms around him and burying her face into his chest.

Her tears flowed heavier now. He rested one hand on her back and stroked her hair. Her floral shampoo tickled his senses. Minutes passed. Her tears slowed, replaced by a sniffle.

"I'm sorry," she said, pulling away. He fought his instinct to hold her in place and continue to stroke her silky hair.

"It is the nature of the match," he said, standing straight. Did his mate not understand this? The female joined the male's clan. The clan provided protection to her and any offspring.

Another sigh. Her shoulders slumped. He did not enjoy seeing her this way. Defeated. "I know," she said. "I just... It is what it is."

"Rest. I will sit with Meridan," he said.

She gave him a skeptical look but eventually nodded.

Mylomon settled onto the floor, legs folded in a meditative position. The floor was uncomfortable and cold. Good. He needed the clarity.

Never one to be shy with words, those same words died on his tongue around Daisy. Nothing he could utter was good enough for her ears. He needed more time before they were matched to plan. Without a plan, an assassin was little more than an impulsive murderer. The option of waiting and planning had been removed. He needed to move forward.

He needed to win his mate's affection. He needed to give her something unique. Something she prized. Treasured. Something as valuable to Daisy as she was to him.

His eyes opened, focusing on the regen tank.

Meridan Vargas floated in a vat of green gel. Her dark hair fanned out from her face, a face which mirrored Daisy's. The sisters were very much alike in appearance and build, only one was dark and the other blonde. Meridan had a pleasing fullness to her hips and thighs. While this did nothing for Mylomon's appetite, he imagined that Daisy shared the same trait, and this roused his appetite.

Speaking of appetite, the medic Kalen had worn himself thin caring for the Terran female. Plus, the two had been on the cusp of romantic relations before the attack. And Meridan had been exempt, but no more.

And today was her birthday.

Meridan needed to be tested. She would be matched

with Kalen. Mylomon had no doubt. A family member needed to authorize the test.

Mylomon unfolded his limbs and rose from the floor. As Meridan's brother-in-law, he needed to have a conversation with a huffy technician.

Yes, this was a good plan.

DAISY

NO ONE WOULD CONFESS TO AUTHORIZING MERIDAN'S test. By no one, Daisy meant Kalen. That arrogant, smug alien doctor would not admit to testing Meridan while she was unconscious and unable to give consent for the procedure. Everyone knew he did. It was obvious with the way he mooned over her and never left medical.

"I guess you got what you wanted," Daisy said, confronting him.

"This is not what I wanted," Kalen replied.

Sure. Whatever. Daisy stuck a hand on her hip and planted her feet, ready for a fight. "I know you authorized the test."

"On my honor, I did not."

That test didn't authorize itself.

Regardless, they were family now. Daisy did not know her sister's stance on being married to an alien. Meridan had always been quiet about her love life and even quieter about her hopes and dreams. Would she be upset? Would her match please her? Daisy honestly had no idea. She did know, however, that Meridan had been attracted to the alien physician. They had flirted and even kissed. It might not be such an unpleasant surprise for Meridan, unlike Daisy's own match.

Daisy got exactly what she wanted: a big, strong alien. Of course her alien was also terrifying. The frightening part of him was more than his physical appearance. He stood taller and broader than all of the other warriors on the base, but it was more than that. His dark complexion allowed him to blend in perfectly with the shadows. He moved silently. Everything about him screamed he was a killer, ready to strike. His features were too sharp to be handsome and his eyes gleamed with a pitiless intelligence. He always observed. Watched. Nothing escaped his attention. That rattled Daisy more than anything.

The way the other Mahdfel skirted around him lead Daisy to believe that he terrified his own kind, too. A secret mission to search out a traitor had brought him to the SCLB. Perhaps the Mahdfel had a good reason to avoid him. So, yeah, she got her big and strong and terrifying alien. That was her man.

Honestly, Daisy liked it. She had the biggest, baddest and scariest warrior. What did that say about her? She knew she had a thing for the muscle-bound aliens. She did not know she would be so attracted to a such a dominating, masculine specimen.

And Mylomon was dominating. When he chose to reveal himself, he filled the room with his presence. It unnerved most people but it made Daisy weak in the knees.

Why did she feel so alone? She wasn't supposed to be alone. Her mate was supposed to cherish and protect her but she went to sleep in an empty apartment and often went days without speaking to him.

Why didn't he ask for sex? Or express at least a little interest in it? Wasn't that the Mahdfel's primary purpose? To make a new generation of little warriors?

For two weeks they shared her little apartment and he slept on the floor in her bedroom. Not once did he try to climb in or even touch her. Did Mylo find her un-attractive? It's not like he hung around to talk or give her a chance to flirt and get his temperature. Not that she wanted to have sex just yet. Yes, he was hot.

Scary but hot.

He strutted around half-naked, showing off a body that would put a god to shame. Her repeated requests for him to wear a damn shirt were meet with that infuriating smirk of his, which lead her to believe he was indeed showing off. Mixed signals, much?

She just had no idea what went in that horned head of his. If this was what married life would be like, she got the short end of the stick.

When Meridan woke, Daisy carefully cleaned the gel off her and tried to explain the situation to her fuzzy headed sister. "The regen tank fixed everything wrong with you," speaking slowly to let the words sink in. "You had some broken ribs, a collapsed lung, and your liver was about to give up the ghost. It worked really well."

"That's good, right?" Meridan's voice rasped, sounding like it scraped along shards of broken glass.

Probably felt that way, too.

"Really, really well."

Meridan shook her head slightly.

"The tank fixed everything that was wrong, including the little stuff and the old stuff." Daisy removed the sheet, exposing Meridan's unblemished skin. Her old scar, the one given to her by a Suhlik during the invasion, was gone.

Daisy continued, "You're not infertile anymore. You were matched. It even took away your freckles."

"My freckles," Meridan said, unbelieving. "I liked my freckles."

When it finally sank in, Meridan was not happy. She insisted on being re-tested. The results remained the same. She was matched Kalen. That wasn't the surprise.

The surprise was how hard it was to say goodbye.

Daisy had had two weeks to prepare herself for this moment. Meridan cried shamelessly. Daisy refused to give in to her tears but did a poor job. She needed her big sister to know that she could to take care of herself. She would to be all right. They were tough nuts, after all.

Mylomon lead her away toward the teleporter.

With Meridan recovered, there was little reason to stay. Walking away, she bit her lower lip to keep the tears contained. As they stood on the teleport platform, his thick finger brushed away the damp tracks on her face in a gesture that was almost tender.

"Are you ready, female?"

Daisy looked down at her feet. He couldn't even say her name she was so repulsive to him. "Sure. Whatever. Let's get this over with."

CHAPTER SIX

DAISY

"FEMALE, REMAIN HERE."

Mylomon dumped her unceremoniously in his quarters and left. Technically it was their shared quarters but the space had a Spartan, hyper masculine vibe. She'd have to work hard to add her own personality to the functional grey rooms.

Daisy focused her attention on the decor rather than her feelings of rejection.

The common room had a sunken conversation pit with a sofa that looked unused. She couldn't imagine Mylomon doing something as ordinary as relaxing and watching a film on the view screen. There was a small table and one chair. One. Empty rooms circled the common room. Well, mostly, if you didn't count the Room of Knives.

She stood in the doorway, a shiver running down her spine. She didn't dare cross the threshold. An extensive collection of knives was mounted on the walls. She hadn't realized there was so much variety in blade size and length. Some must be daggers but Daisy didn't know the technical difference that distinguished a dagger from a plain old knife.

She found an empty sleeping room, and another. The bed was sunk into the floor, much like in the common room. It would be cozy if not for the stark colors and brutal functionality. The sheets scratched, like fabric softener technology hadn't been discovered by aliens. Finally, she found what must be the master bedroom. At first glance, she thought it empty as well but noticed a half-full glass of water next to the bed, the only sign of life in the barren environment.

Daisy slumped against the walls and slid down to the floor. That was her marriage bed, scratchy sheets and all. She mentally added color to the space with pillows, plants, and decorative items on the wall other than, you know, knives. What could she even do to make the room less oppressive? New linens and a landscape painting could only go so far.

Decorating. Yeah, right. Like that would fix anything. Daisy's laughter verged on hysterical and then dissolved into tears. She was alone on a battle cruiser full of alien warriors with a mate that couldn't stand her. He'd left the first available moment, dumping her in this sterile grey suite of rooms. So what if her tears were full of self-pity? It was her pity party and she'd cry if she wanted. All she needed was a tub of ice cream and a cheesy movie.

The comm unit beeped with an incoming message. Daisy ignored it but the volume increased until the point she had to answer or dismiss the call.

It was Vox.

"What do you want, fly boy?" Using voice only she could hide her red eyes and dripping nose but the unevenness in her voice betrayed her.

"I possess a double caramel white chocolate raspberry peppermint mocha latte with your name on it. Open the door."

Daisy stuck out her tongue and mock gagged. "That sounds disgusting. Did you hit every button on the machine or something? Wait. Open the door? Where are you."

"Open the door and find out."

Daisy raced to the front door, throwing herself at Vox. He held up his arms to avoid spilling the coffee. "I'm so glad you're here!"

"Careful. Why don't you drink your abomination of caffeine and sugar before it gets cold?"

The double caramel white chocolate raspberry peppermint mocha latte was a cacophony of sickening sweet flavors. She loved it. Sugary coffee: an acceptable substitute when there was no ice cream to be had.

"This is your new clan?"

He nodded and peered over her shoulder. "Is your mate home?"

"No. Do you want to come in."

"I cannot be alone with another's mate, not until—" He motioned to the spot where his neck joined his shoulders.

Daisy's eyes went wide. Right. Not until she was claimed. Fat chance of that happening anytime soon. "Don't want to challenge Mylomon for me?"

"You are my heart sister and I love you, but no.

Come to the lounge with me and I will show you the fancy coffee machine."

"And I can press all the buttons?"

"Don't you always?"

Perhaps it was the sugar or the caffeine but Vox lifted her mood. She wasn't alone. She had a friend and an ally.

Functional grey walls lined the wide corridors of the *Judgment*. The walls had a gentle curve, giving the space an organic, flowing feel. Even the hallways felt more inviting than Mylomon's quarters.

Warriors studied Daisy as they moved past. "Why are they looking at me like that?"

"They are curious."

"Never seen a human before?"

"Curious as to who matched the foundling. After word got out that I knew you, the questions never ceased."

A dozen questions crowded her mind. "What's a foundling?"

Vox headed toward an open space with lounge furniture, plants and a bar. The far wall held a floor to ceiling window, offering a view of the stars as the

Judgment made progress toward the next mission. The aroma of coffee and hot beverages floated through the air. Daisy made a beeline to the coffee machine. She dumped her terribly sweet atrocity and made herself a fresh latte with a reasonable amount of caramel.

"Have you ever wondered why the Mahdfel insist on keeping our mates and children close to us? Even when we go into battle?" Vox asked.

"I always found it a bit weird. The human military allow families to live together on or near a base but not in an active combat zone. They certainly don't live on a battle cruiser." Steaming cup in hand, she settled into a comfortable looking chair.

Vox settled into the chair across from her. "The Suhlik continue their genetic engineering. They attack settlements, kill families and steal away children. We keep our mates close because otherwise they would be targets."

"Defenseless."

"Yes. Even so, occasionally the Suhlik are able to penetrate our defenses and they snatch a Mahdfel son."

Daisy had a hard time imagining why the Suhlik would do that. Weren't there enough defenseless planets for the Suhlik to invade, like they had on Earth?

Targeting the Mahdfel seemed like an unreasonable amount of work for little reward.

"The Suhlik continue their *research*," he spat out the word. Daisy had never heard such venom in his voice. "They *alter* the child. Occasionally, a clan may find these research facilities and rescue the stolen children."

"Foundlings."

He nodded.

Daisy stared into the slowly dissolving foam of her drink. "You said they were curious about the foundling's match. Is Mylo—"

"Yes."

That was garbage in so many ways. Mylomon's family was murdered. He was stolen. Experimented on. "You said they were altered. Altered how?"

"I am not sure."

She nodded. Mylomon was so much bigger than the other warriors: taller, broader built, even more musclebound than the average Mahdfel male. If the Mahdfel were super soldiers, perhaps the Suhlik tried to forge Mylomon into a super-super soldier.

"The clan does not trust your mate," Vox said.

"Why not? I thought he was the warlord's second?"

"The warlord trusts him but the other warriors... Foundlings, even adult foundlings, make us nervous."

"Even you?" Nervous. So unspecific.

He gave a noncommittal shrug. Such a human gesture. "I am not sure."

"So what's your point? You show up to let me know my husband has a tragic past and the clan doesn't accept him? What did you hope to achieve here?"

"You needed to know all the facts."

"You didn't give me facts, Vox. You gave me gossip and rumors." Daisy leaned back in the chair. "I'm happy to see you. God knows I need a friend but I'm not going to gossip about my husband." She couldn't account for the urge to defend Mylomon. The male barely spoke to her and gave her no reason to regard him with affection but she didn't like the idea that his clan, the foundation of Mahdfel culture, failed to trust him. And all for something beyond his control that had happened to him as a child.

"There was another point to my visit," he said.

"Oh? Going to share new ways to ostracize my mate?"

Vox's brows knitted. "The large, flightless bird with the buried head?"

"Are you even being serious right now?" Her patience wore thin. Too much had happened in the last twenty-four hours, her emotions were swinging from one extreme to another. "Look, I'm just tired and cranky."

"Ah." He moved as if to pat her on the knee but pulled his hand back. Right. No touching another male's mate. "I have good news for you."

"I can use some. Sock it to me, fly boy."

"I learned today that the medic Kalen is also part of this clan."

Daisy dropped the coffee and threw herself at Vox, wrapping her arms around him in a tight embrace. Kalen was here, which meant Meridan would be here. She had her sister again. And their brother. The gang was back together. "That's the best news! Always start with that. I swear, sometimes I think you have rocks in your head."

Vox gave a stiff pat on her back before pushing her away. "I appreciate your enthusiasm but I can't participate in such a display—"

"With another male's mate. I know. I don't need you to participate. I'm going to hug you and you can't stop me."

"Fine, if you must, make the me victim then of your affection." He held both arms above his head as he suffered the indignity of her hugs, a smile on his lips.

MYLOMON

HIS CLAN CONSPIRED TO KEEP HIM SEPARATED FROM his mate. The males wanted details about his new mate. The warlord had only recently allowed the clan to register to be genetically matched to potential brides. The previous warlord forbade it. As a result, the clan aboard the *Judgment* was comprised of single males all eager for their match. And eager to gossip about another male's mate. Paax allowed the men to register in waves to better allow the female to be absorbed into the clan. The *Judgment*, as fine of a battle cruiser as it was, lacked many refinements and comforts. Paax's mate, the Terran Mercy, had insisted on several improvements to make the battlecruiser more habitable to females.

Seeran, in particular, vexed Mylomon. The chief of security made demands of his time and Mylomon was in no mood to entertain him. He barely slowed his pace to let the other male's shorter legs keep up.

"I require a briefing of your mission," Seeran said.

"And have you discussed your requirements with our warlord?"

"As chief of security, I demand to be kept abreast of all variables which threaten the safety of the clan."

Mylomon paused, aligning his great frame with Seeran. He did not disagree. If the roles were reversed, Mylomon would be making demands for information. As it happened, he already made a full report to the warlord. If Paax wanted Seeran to know, he would already know.

"It is not your place to make demands of me," Mylomon said. Seeran held his burning gaze. The male's bright magenta complexion did not discolor or fade. Impressive. "Unless you wish to challenge me?"

Seeran's gaze remained steady. "No, sir. Not today."

A grin threatened to crack the fierce scowl on his

face. Seeran had balls. Too bad the males were nothing like friends because Mylomon could respect him.

Mylomon walked away, thumping Seeran's shoulder as he passed.

Daisy waited for him in their quarters.

He anticipated she would find the space lacking. He found it lacking but had not the time nor the inclination when he was single to make his quarters more comfortable. He was a genetic abomination. No match would ever be found for him so why bother to prepare for a female who did not exist? Now he cursed that lazy, short-sighted fool.

Immediately upon arrival, the warlord had summoned Mylomon. He deposited his mate and sent the warrior Vox to attend to her. Vox was the male who accompanied Daisy to the ball on the night of the attack. Mylomon sensed no attraction between them, only friendship, so he fought down his bitter jealousy and let another male comfort his wife.

Finally, at the end of a seemingly endless barrage of urgent requests, he returned to his quarters and spend his off duty time with his wife. He would not arrive empty handed. He stopped in the mess hall and bought a meal. Feeding his mate on SCLB had been necessary. She would not leave medical bay, not for hunger and not for exhaustion. Through trial and error, he brought her various Terran foods, taking careful note of what she ate, picked at and skipped altogether. He anticipated that she would enjoy the meal he brought. He heard her speak of longing for tacos so he made sure that the Mess could produce the Terran edible.

Daisy scented the air the moment he arrived, her funny little nose twitching. "What is that?"

"Food."

"I need it now. Give me." Her words ran together with enthusiasm. She took the tray from him and set it on the small table. She immediately began to assemble protein and shredded vegetables in a corn wrapper. The table barely had enough surface area for the tray, let alone two people eating from plates. He assumed that was how his mate would prefer to consume her food. Terrans insisted on certain rituals pertaining to meals. He needed a larger table.

"I will requisition a more suitable table for you, female."

"Hmm?" She added a spicy sauce to the item in her hand. "Sounds great. Have you ever had a taco before?" She held out the item.

He shook his head.

"Have this one. Chicken in a soft shell is good but for whatever reason, I prefer the crummy crispy shells and ground beef. Papi is always going on about it not being authentic. But he lives in the mountains without electricity so what does he know?" She jiggled her hand, waiting for him to take the taco.

"Food is food," he said, taking the item. "And it is not right for the female to feed the male."

"Just eat, grumpy pants."

He had no idea how or why she determined the mood of his pants. Terrans were strange in what they considered noteworthy.

He bit into the taco, the warm outside layer giving way to the spicy interior. The protein and plant material had competing textures which proved surprisingly pleasant. The sauce possessed a zing. He nodded his approval.

Smiling with satisfaction, Daisy assembled her own. He copied her motions but was not as quick or graceful. The contents slid out of his first attempt. He growled and she laughed good naturedly at his frustration.

The sweet, light sound of her laughter pleased him. It meant that she could find joy with him. And the fact that she laughed at his misfortune meant that she was not frightened of him. A female should not be frightened of her male.

After the meal and depositing the dishes in the recycler, Daisy yawned.

"Sleep now, female," he said, leading her to the sleeping room.

"It has been a long day." Bleary eyed she pawed through her bag to retrieve a sleeping shirt. It was the Mahdfel custom to sleep nude, a custom he wished for her to pick up sooner rather than later. She'd worn that infernal shirt for the last two weeks. While the lace trim fell mid-thigh and created a pleasing image, he'd rather know his mate was comfortable and not constrained by unnecessary fabric.

He thought of her comfort only, of course.

"Wait, this is the master bedroom," Daisy said, suddenly away of their location.

"This is my bed," he said. "You are my mate."

Daisy nodded. He could see the flutter of her racing

pulse in her delicate neck. Her pink tongue licked her lower lip. She responded with desire to the absolute certainty in his voice. "But you never tried to get into bed with me before."

"That was *your* bed. You did not invite me."

Daisy blushed a pretty pink and slapped a hand over her mouth. "I'm such a bitch."

He frowned, displeased at her words. He brushed back the hair from her face and held her gaze. "No one speaks ill of my wife, not even my wife."

She nodded. "I wasn't even mad at you, not really. Just distracted. And I made you sleep on the *floor*. Like a dog." Then, in a quiet voice, "Like a monster."

"You are as the stars made you," he said.

"Did you just agree that I'm a bitch?" Her tone edged away from playful and into distraught.

"Your concern for your sister blinded you," he said, stroking her arm. "As it happened, you spent many nights sleeping in a chair in medical. I slept in your bed then."

She took a step back, hand on hip and grinned up at him. Expecting. Mylomon arched an eyebrow. "Well," she said, "are you going to invite *me*?"

"All that I have is yours. You do not need to ask."

Daisy motioned to him to turn around while she changed into the ridiculous sleeping shirt. So needlessly shy. He had yet to see his mate nude but he knew she was breathtaking. He would enjoy exploring the perfection of her form but not tonight. Not yet.

He stripped down and sank down to the bed.

"You're naked," she said.

"As I have been every night," he replied.

"Well, yeah, but we weren't in the same bed." Her voice sounded strained. He studied the warm flush spreading across her face, chest and the apex of her thighs. He listened to her quickening pulse. Desire. Anticipation.

Mylomon wanted to shout with victory that his mate found him desirable but this was not the time. Daisy remained skittish. An unexpected outburst could frighten her away.

Would it? Had Daisy demonstrated herself to be a timid female frightened of her own shadow? No. His mate was far from that. She had fire in her blood.

Mylomon moved quicker than a rumor and pressed Daisy against the mattress, his form above her. He nuzzled the curve where her neck joined her shoulder. This is the spot where he would mark her. He licked the skin, letting her flavors burst over his tongue.

Her eyes grew wide. "What are you doing?"

"You taste sweet, wife, just as I knew you would."

She shifted underneath him. Not a struggle. Everything in her body told him that she enjoyed this. Wanted more. Her nipples pebbled beneath the thin cotton shirt. Her breathing grew erratic. A plea for attention, then.

"Do not fear me, female. I will not touch you until you are ready." He rolled away, leaving her alone to one side.

She panted for a moment before regaining herself, hand resting on her chest. "Perhaps you should fear me."

"Good night, female."

"Good night, Mylo."

CHAPTER SEVEN

DAISY

BEING MATCHED MEANT NEVER BEING ALONE, AT least that's how Daisy understood it. She'd have her big, strong alien warrior to protect her always and she'd never be alone. So why did she feel more isolated than ever?

She'd gotten her big, strong alien but he was also the tiniest bit terrifying. By "tiny" she meant huge. He was completely terrifying. He had no friends, as far as she could tell, and he made his clan nervous. How scary do you have to be to frighten an army of fierce warriors?

Sometimes he would be in the room and she couldn't tell, his breathing so quiet as to be cloaked in silence. And he moved so quietly that he snuck up on her. She'd turn around with a start, finding him right behind her.

Yup, that was her husband: big, strong, silent and scary in the dark.

The strange thing wasn't that Mylomon frightened her. She felt safe in his presence. If he was the scariest thing in the universe, then he'd chase away the other scary things.

Being surreptitiously watched from the shadows by her scary husband was, oddly, not the same as having him with her. Humans craved companionship. Daisy reminded herself it was normal, healthy even, to feel little pangs of disappointment when she woke up in the massive bed alone. Her companion only crept in during the night and vanished again before the alarm rang. So far, if this was married life, it sucked.

The day after Daisy arrived on the *Judgment*, Meridan and Kalen arrived. The day after, normalcy settled in. The hums and whirrs of the ship were normal. Sleeping next to her purple alien husband was normal.

Listening to his even breaths was normal. And waking up alone felt normal.

It sucked.

"I require you to clean these instruments, not scrub them into oblivion," Kalen snapped. He took the surgical instrument out of her hands and gave Daisy a box full of med kits. "Let your idle hands re-stock these."

Daisy rolled her eyes but cracked open the first kit. The expected contents were present and well before their expiration dates. Busy work. The male gave her busy work. Still, it was better than being stuck in that unwelcoming apartment by herself.

"Sorry," Meridan said, opening her own busy work kit.

"You'd think he'd be nicer so, you know, you'd *want* to clean his instrument."

Meridan blushed.

It took Daisy a moment to account for her sister's blush. She didn't mean... Stars. Oh well. Better go with it. "So, have you?"

"Have I what?"

"Cleaned his instrument?"

The contents of the kit became fascinating to Meridan.

Daisy didn't want to needle her sister. Well, maybe a little. New normal, right? And what was more normal than your little sister giving you grief? "I don't know how you live with that," she said.

"He's not so bad," Meridan said. She carefully checked the expiration date on the contents. Satisfied, she repacked the kit.

"He's a condescending, foul-tempered, mean-spirited dick."

A smile tugged at the corner of Meridan's lips. "Oh... So that's how the cool kids define 'bad' nowadays? I can't keep up with the lingo. Then yes. He's bad."

"Seriously, how can you sit there all smiles and rainbows? I mean, you hear how he talks to us, right? Like we're simpletons good only for busy work and not highly skilled professionals?"

"Mmm." She opened another kit and emptied out of the contents. "Look, I know he's all snarls and barks on the outside but underneath it all he's—"

"A new and exciting layer of snarls and barks?"

"A marshmallow. He's sweet." Daisy gave her sister

a look. "Honestly. Of course, just when I'm getting all warm and fuzzy he opens big fat mouth and ruins it."

Daisy giggled.

Kalen stomped over, exchanging the completed kits with new ones. "Females! Are you here to work or to socialize?"

Daisy giggled harder as the physician stomped away. "Sourpuss," she said.

Meridan shrugged. "It's not you. It's me."

"What a load of baloney."

"No, seriously. I had to fight him to get out of our quarters today. If he had his way, I'd never leave the bed. I told him that work was the only way I would build my muscle tone back up."

Daisy rolled her eyes. "Medical gave you the all clear yesterday. You're not an invalid."

"So he's over protective." Then, "I am a little tired, not that I'd ever admit it to him. How about you? How's the married life?"

Daisy reached for a new kit. "I guess Mylo's really busy. I haven't seen him much."

"Really?" Meridan stopped working, focusing her attention on her little sister. "I thought the biological imperative to, ah..." Her voice trailed off and she blushed. Talking about sex with her your sister was hard, no matter how old you were.

"Well, it doesn't seem to bother him too much." It bothered her. They'd been married on paper for more than two weeks and he *still* had not claimed her. Was there something wrong with her?

No. Daisy shoved that thought right out. The timing was wrong. How could he come sniffing around her bed with her sister floating in a regen tank, near death? It was considerate the way he did not pressure her for sex.

But they were back on his ship. Her sister was fine. He could pressure her now. She'd even welcome a little pressure. More than welcome. Enthusiastically get all on it.

"These things take time," Meridan said. Concern darkened her eyes. Her sister's face, so familiar, had been altered subtly by the regen tank, but that look of concern remained the same.

"You know," Daisy said, forcing brightness into her voice, "I just can't get over you not having freckles. It's weird. You're you but not."

"I don't feel like myself." Meridan patted her chest

and waved vaguely at the rest of her body. "This is weird."

Daisy reached across the table and grabbed her hand. "The whole situation is weird but I'm glad you're here."

Meridan's eyes softened and she gave a meager smile. "As long as we're together, we're never alone, right?"

* * *

NEVER ALONE, RIGHT? DAISY FELT MORE ALONE THAN ever.

Three weeks and Mylomon *still* hadn't claimed her. The Mahdfel didn't wait, she heard from other wives. They were the kiss first, get to know you later kind of guys.

At first the waiting to claim her seemed sweet. Considerate, even. Now the lack of sex made her nervous. Did he not want her? Did he find her un-attractive? She wanted him. The whole situation was pure frustration. She was a healthy girl with a healthy appetite.

Maybe he if was home more they'd have a chance

to talk about it, but he was never home. She hadn't figured out his schedule yet. He came and left at all hours, seemingly without a pattern. Second-in-command was a prestigious position. Perhaps an unstable work schedule came with the rank. Not that he told her when he left or when to expect him back. Why would Mylomon share that information with his wife? He behaved as if he expected her to sit and wait in their quarters all day, which was complete garbage, by the way.

Working the last week in the medical bay with Kalen and Meridan only highlighted the problems in their marriage. Meridan and Kalen seemed to have reached an accord. Meridan smiled and hummed under her breath when she thought no one was paying attention. Kalen's barking demeanor had softened. Well, he remained rude and arrogant as all get out, but he listened to Meridan's, and Daisy's, professional opinions.

Daisy had even met the warlord and his human bride, Mercy. Half-way through her pregnancy, Mercy frequently visited medical. Every ache or slight discomfort sent the warlord into a frenzy of concern. Including Mercy's mother, there were only four human women on board. The Mahdfel simply had no experience in what to expect from a Terran-Mahdfel pregnancy. While her sister was the obstetrics specialist, Daisy was more than willing to serve as a shield between a pregnant woman and an overly concerned warlord.

Daisy did not miss the genuine affection Paax displayed for his wife, or the warmth in Mercy's eyes when she squeezed his hands. Their love was obvious and sweet.

It annoyed her.

And Meridan and Kalen, while not overly affectionate, were clearly getting along. They'd probably done the claiming ceremony already. Jealousy stabbed at her heart. She should be happy her sister got along with her unexpected alien husband but she only felt bitterness because her own husband continued to avoid her.

The entire situation annoyed Daisy. She wasn't the kind of girl to sit and wait around all day for scraps of her husband's frosty attention. And she also wasn't the kind of girl to sit around and feel sorry for herself. Unhappy? Do something about it. That's what a Vargas did. The frosty situation with Mylo made her unhappy and she intended on doing something to fix the situation.

Assess and adapt, right? Hard work gave her focus and control of the situation, so it was fair to say that Mylo walked into a trap that morning.

She waited at the small kitchenette table. She prepared—fetched from the mess hall—two plates of eggs with a bacon-type product she saw him eat once and coffee. Lots of coffee.

Mylomon entered their quarters. He paused, sniffing the air. Daisy pushed a plate forward while sipping from her mug of coffee.

"What is this?"

"Breakfast. Join me." She pushed the plate another inch across the table. With a grunt he joined her at the table. He ate unceremoniously, shoveling the almost-bacon into his mouth. Charming.

"I'm not happy," she said.

Mylomon stopped chewing, his eyes watching her carefully. She had no idea what he was thinking and that was the problem.

"I'm not happy because I don't know you."

"You know me."

"No, I don't. Do you have a favorite food? Movie?"

"Food is food. I don't have a preference. Films are a waste of time," he said, resuming the shoveling of the almost-bacon.

Three entire sentences... that was progress, right? "What about hobbies? When you're not, I don't know, stabbing things, what do you do to relax?"

He drained the cup of coffee in one go. Graceful meal companion he was not. "I like knives." He waved to the far wall, to his displayed knife collection.

Of course he did. Daisy turned to look at the wall of sharpness. Mounted on the wall, a bluish light illuminating each knife of his collection. "Well," she said, "we should have a date night."

He paused in the shoveling. "What is a date night?"

"It means that when I get off my shift at the medical bay, I want to spend time with you. We can have dinner and do something fun."

His eyebrows shot up.

"Not sex," she said quickly but she knew she'd cave if he expressed the slightest interest. "I'm not the kind of girl who puts out on the first date."

"Is this part of the human mating custom?" he finally asked.

"Yes."

"We're already married."

"So we're doing it out of order. Deal. I'm *trying* to build a bridge here. Are you going to help me or are you going to rain on my parade?"

He said nothing. She watched the muscle in his jaw clench and unclench as he worked through her question. Finally, "I have no idea what that idiom means."

"It means when I return in eight hours, we're going to spend our recreation time together. You pick. We can do something you like." Polish knife blades or practice stabbing things, she guessed.

"I'm in charge of date night?"

"I made breakfast. Equal distribution of work."

"You brought this from the mess hall."

The alarm on her wrist comm beeped. Time to go. She stood up from the table and leaned in for a kiss but stopped short. Instead she awkwardly patted Mylo on the shoulder. "I'll be home at eight. Surprise me."

MYLOMON

HE NEEDED GUIDANCE. BRIGHT ENOUGH TO KNOW when he was out of his depths, everything about his

Terran mate was so far out of his depths the pressure paralyzed him. Bright enough to say this to his mate?

No. The shyness that crippled him to inaction continued to plague him. The situation was unreasonable for a warrior of his rank. He served as second-in-command of a clan. The warlord relied on him to solve problems. He had been the victor of countless battles and yet this small Terran woman paralyzed him. Just the simple act of speaking to her was daunting. The same questions that plagued him the first night he saw her continued to vex him now. What would he say to her? What could they possibly have to talk about?

How was your day, dear?

I crushed the larynx of a crewman who questioned the warlord's fitness to lead. If he so much as mumbles an insubordinate word again, I will slit his throat. What's for dinner?

No. None of that seemed appropriate to say to his sunny, eager mate. If he shared his activities with his mate, she would be horrified. She had already called him a monster once in anger. If she discovered his true nature and learned that he really was a monster...

He couldn't finish the thought. He would lose her forever.

The skin on Mylomon's chest burned in frustration.

She was unhappy *now*. He was losing her *now*. There was no good solution. He needed guidance.

But who to speak with? The warlord? Paax appeared to have a solid relationship with his mate. Mylomon knew the warlord loved his Terran mate, had loved her almost instantly, and he was certain Mercy loved Paax in return. Mylomon would benefit from Paax's wisdom.

There was the small problem of Mercy despising Mylomon. His stabbing her probably had something to do with their lack of affinity. He did not excuse or regret his actions. They were necessary. Mylomon had followed the orders of the previous warlord. His actions brought Paax back to the clan—to seek medical care for his injured mate—and ultimately to challenge and defeat the corrupt warlord Omas. Even if Paax's mate did not have a warm regard for the assassin, he had nothing to regret. Still, seeking Paax's counsel would bring up more problems than it would solve.

The medic Kalen? He had a Terran mate, his mate's sister, in fact. Perhaps the medic would have some insight into pleasing a mate.

Mylomon thought back to the last private

encounter he'd had with the medic. It had ended with punches being thrown.

Perhaps not.

The list of potential mentors shrank. Other members of the clan with mates? No. His current rank and history of being the assassin would create an uncomfortable situation. He had no close friends. He'd never considered his lack of friends to be a detriment but now he reconsidered that position. A friend would be helpful.

The pilot Vox? New to the clan, the male would have no long standing grudge. Plus, he was a friend of Daisy.

Yes. This was the correct male to seek out.

The computer located the pilot. He was currently in a simulation, presumably to familiarize himself with the clan's shuttles and fighters. Mylomon approved of his work ethic.

The pilot removed his visor. Images of scantily clad, bouncing Terran females flickered across the inside screen before vanishing.

Mylomon raised an eyebrow. "That does not appear to be work related."

"Bikini Beach Race 2525, sir," Vox said, removing the simulation gear from his hands. "Helps keep my reflexes sharp."

"And the bouncing females?"

"Motivation."

Displeasure rumbled in his chest but he could not reprimand the pilot. Simulation training to maintain reflexes was an approved activity. He just could not recall an instance of a crew member using Bikini Beach Race 2525. That particular simulation was not prohibited.

An image of his mate clad in only the fabric scraps and bouncing in celebration crowded his thoughts...

Yes. He would be very motivated.

"Can I help you, sir?" Vox stood at attention.

Insecurity gnawed at the edges Mylomon's mind. Had Vox seen his Daisy bounce? He would squeeze the life out of the pilot's beating heart if the answer displeased him.

Peace. He needed information. *Then* he could end the pilot's life if he so much as had a lascivious thought about Daisy.

And still the male smiled at Mylomon like an empty headed fool. Well, pilots needed fast reflexes, not quick wit. Thinking slowed them down.

"I seek your advice."

"Me, sir?" Confusion settled over the pilot's face, brows knitted together. He had adopted Terran habits, it seemed.

"You have spent much time with Terrans."

"Yes, sir. I liked them. They're funny. And bouncy."

Another rumble. "I do not care if they are funny. I seek guidance about my mate."

"Ah." Nervousness replaced confusion. The pilot had information he did not wish to share.

"I will not ask you to break a confidence," Mylomon said, taking a wild stab. Daisy considered the male a friend and would share grievances with him. The other male relaxed, confirming his suspicions. "My mate has requested a date night."

"Sir?"

"I do not know what Daisy expects or would enjoy. Advise me." Mylomon folded his arms over his chest, waiting.

Vox stroked his chin. "Well... Daisy likes to spend time with the people she cares about. She's probably not wanting much."

Mylomon snorted. He had already spent plenty of

time in her company already. That did not please her. It pleased him, however. He could watch her all day, studying the waves of her dark blonde hair. Or mapping the freckles sprinkled across the bridge of her nose. "She specifically requested an activity," he said.

"Ah. In the past we have shared meals."

"We have already shared a meal."

"A special meal. Out, as Terrans say."

"We eat out at the mess hall, with the rest of the crew." The pilot's suggestions were terrible.

"She enjoys *sushi*. It is a roll of rice grains and protein or vegetable in a dried seaweed wrapper."

"She eats seaweed?" He didn't bother to hide his disgust.

Vox shrugged. "The taste is mild but the texture is strange. Squishy."

"I will not consume squishy bland Terran food. Give me another example."

"I have not even told you about the uncooked *tuna*. Once I saw her eat an entire plate —"

"Enough! Sharing a meal is not a viable option."

"She enjoys films."

"Films are a waste of time," Mylomon grumbled.

"Perhaps, but spending time with your mate is not.

And a film is usually two Terran hours. You can sit at her side, holding her hand." Mylomon gave a warning rumbled. "And there is popped corn. She enjoys consuming the exploded kernels coated in butter and salt. Once we went to a film screening in a biome. The film projected onto a screen and we sat on a blanket on the grass. Meridan brought *chocolate chip cookies*." Vox patted his stomach in fond recollection. "Daisy enjoyed that evening very much. You should do the same."

Vox had his full attention. Mylomon took notes as the male gave a detailed report of the date night.

CHAPTER EIGHT

DAISY

DAISY WAS ON THE HUNT.

An experienced hunter understood the value of good equipment. During the dark days of the invasion, the Vargas family had lived in the wilds of the Poconos Mountains. While her sister had preferred to gather berries and root vegetables, Daisy had hunted.

Her father took her on hunting trips before the invasion. At first it was an excuse to spend time with her papa. Then it became taking pride in a skill. Too slight to tolerate the kick back from a rifle or shotgun,

Daisy learned to hunt with a bow. Then it became a matter of survival. She brought in pheasant, grouse, quail, and chukar when she could find it. Once she bagged a wild turkey, but mostly through luck than any real skill. That morning her set-up was a joke and she didn't wait patiently in a blind, instead stumbling through the brush. That turkey was slow and she was quick to draw her bow. It was a sloppy hit, striking the wing but the second arrow hit the bird in the head, a killing blow. Pride wanted her to leave the sloppy kill and let the scavengers take it but she couldn't waste food because of pride. They'd already had too many hungry days.

Daisy would not flub the set-up tonight.

She selected the perfect little black dress. She bought it last year with no particular purpose other than it looked amazing on her and a girl needed a little black dress.

This dress, in particular, had a pencil skirt which hugged her curves in just the right way. The front had a clever starburst cut out revealing a good amount of cleavage but not too much. The hem stopped just above the knee, which was the most flattering length for her legs and she paired it with simple, nude colored ballet flats. Her sister called the dress tasteless. Daisy called it perfect.

She straightened her golden blonde hair and let it hang down her back. Make up was minimal but she found the perfect shade of red lipstick: not too dark, not too bright but a classic red.

Properly equipped for the hunt, Daisy was ready to track down her man. Mylomon thought he could avoid his wife. She didn't know what his deal was. He desired her. She knew that. She desired him. He knew that, right? If not, she planned to make it perfectly clear.

Daisy refused to passively sit back and hope her marriage magically improved. She wasn't helpless. Her skills fed her family during the invasion. Her medical skills saved lives. She had the power to forge her marriage into a shape that made her happy.

The first step was getting Mylomon on board.

A warrior, Seeran, with a bright magenta complexion, escorted her to the ship's orchard.

Neat rows of fruit bearing trees filled the long, narrow room. Real growing grass carpeted the floor. An open irrigation system ran down the center, like a brook. The far wall was constructed of translucent, high strength material, like a window. One panel flickered white, like a movie screen.

Then Daisy noticed the blanket and picnic hamper.

"Thank you," she said, carefully arranging herself on the blanket. The tight fitting dress restricted her movement. "How soon will Mylo arrive?"

"He said he would be on his way when he sent me."

Good.

Alone in the orchard, Daisy peeked into the hamper. There was a bowl of popcorn. Chocolate chip cookies. Two bottles of beer. Sandwiches. She recognized the menu. Mylo talked to Vox. What he lacked in creativity he compensated with thoughtfulness.

Daisy ate a handful of popcorn and waited. And waited. The movie began to play. Excitement flared in her heart and she looked around for Mylomon but she was alone. She checked her comm unit for missed message. Nothing.

The movie played, a twentieth century super-hero movie about a rich playboy in a suit of power armor. Probably not the most romantic choice, but romance didn't seem to matter much as the moment. Every minute Mylomon didn't show was another wound to her heart.

She was *trying*, dang it. She wanted a happy marriage. She wanted to curl up next to her husband in bed at night, safe and secure. She wanted to smile when she saw his face first thing in the morning. She wanted kids, snotty noses, chaotic mornings, and sleepless nights with crying babies. The whole deal.

He had to meet her halfway. She couldn't do this on her own.

And she was very much on her own.

End credits rolled. The movie lasted just over two hours and no Mylomon.

She got stood up.

Daisy pushed herself off the ground in an ungraceful maneuver but she didn't care. She was a bit beyond caring about appearances now. Her own husband stood her up. No message. No sending another warrior to let her know he was late or tied up. The rational side of her understood that he had responsibilities and some crisis came up that required his attention. No one else would do. The clan needed him and who was she to throw a temper tantrum because she didn't get all the attention she craved?

The rest of her was furious. He didn't even send a text message. How busy could he be that he couldn't say, "Computer, send a message to Daisy. Running late. Don't eat all the popcorn without me."

He couldn't even take ten seconds to send her a message. That's how little she mattered to him.

She couldn't do this on her own.

Screw him and his interesting face.

She *wouldn't* do this on her own.

Divorce happened. They were rare with human-Mahdfel marriages but they happened. She still had that option. As long as he didn't claim her, they didn't have sex, she could file for divorce.

Nausea churned her stomach. She didn't like that idea. Hated it, actually. Not being with Mylomon felt wrong but she couldn't stay with a man who had no respect for her. And standing her up on date night? His actions spoke louder than any words.

She didn't want to be divorced. She wanted to be married. To Mylomon, surprisingly.

Maybe she could stay with Meridan and Kalen for a few days, until she cooled down. Their quarters probably had empty rooms to spare. The thought of being around the happy couple during work and off hours gave her pause. Could she take that much sweetness?

Maybe she could move into an empty suit of rooms. The *Judgment* was huge. There had to be room to spare. If she asked the warlord's wife, Mercy, she'd get a sympathetic ear. Daisy had only known Mercy for a week and she understood that Mercy and Mylo did not get along.

Imagine that, Mylomon not getting along with a woman.

Disgusted with him and her own dashed expectations, Daisy returned to their quarters. She didn't know what she would say to him. Nothing nice. If he didn't slink home until the morning she might be calm enough to discuss the situation.

If he stumbled in sooner... She wasn't sure what she'd do. Cry. Yell. Hide away in the bedroom.

MYLOMON

WHILE SERVING AS THE WARLORD'S ASSASSIN, THE CLAN ignored him. He lurked in the background and avoided close scrutiny. His time was his own, to spend as he pleased.

The new warlord, Paax, elevated Mylomon's position to his second-in-command. Paax informed him it was punishment for Mylomon's part in the mutiny against the old warlord. Omas had been cruel, which a proper Mahdfel warrior would endure with stoicism. What was cruelty in the grand scheme of things? The Suhlik were worse and the Mahdfel would persevere. An experimental rejuvenation treatment had twisted the warlord and left him insane. When the warlord lost his own mate, he prohibited the warriors from being matched. The clan's vitality and strength diminished. They needed a new warlord. Was it Mylomon's fault that Paax refused to confront the monster he created in Omas? No, but it was Mylomon who engineered events to bring down the insane warlord.

And Paax had a long memory. There was no chore too menial for his second. No job too tedious. Tasks better delegated to others were given to Mylomon, and he performed each without a grumble. Astro-Nav needed a consultation? Mylomon was there with the information the navigators needed. Unusual readings from Engineering? Send Mylomon. The task list was endless.

In all fairness, his abilities were well suited to address the issue in Engineering. What would normally be a complex task of disassembling a panel and crawling through an access tube was a simple matter of him phasing through a wall and following the engineer's instructions.

The clan's curiosity about his mate compounded his irritation. Their constant *questions* about Terran females slowed down his efficiency in completing his assignments, and thus returning to his mate. It was as if they had never seen a Terran woman before.

He knew the real reason. It was hope.

If an aberration such as Mylomon could find his match, then it was only a matter of time before they were matched to their mates.

He did not want to be the clan's beacon of hope. He wanted to have a date night with his mate.

The warlord was less than impressed with Mylomon's observation. Paax paced the length of his ready room, his one remaining horn glinting in the light. The other, sacrificed when he challenged Omas, grew back slowly.

"It seems we both dislike having responsibilities thrust upon us," Paax said.

Mylomon did not regret the part he played in Paax's challenge and defeat of the previous warlord. "I would do nothing different."

The warlord nodded and called up a holographic map. Mylomon did not recognize the planet but the features were familiar. "The clan requires us to assume many roles. Some we relish. Some are a burden. Others a chance to triumph against overwhelming odds. It is the challenge of being a warrior. The females we care about will see beneath these facades to our true selves."

If Daisy saw his true self, she would recoil in disgust. Underneath all the posturing of honor and rank and duty, Mylomon was monster.

Paax studied Mylomon, brow knitted as if he knew his did not bridge the divide between them. "The clan has need of your unique skills."

"Here?" Mylomon leaned forward to study the map.

"We've located a signal here," Paax said, pointing to a glowing green location. "But there is a second signal. I need you to pursue it." A second green point flared on the holographic planet's surface. "It will take you away from your mate for some time."

"You don't ask for much, do you? As I recall, when you were matched, you were not separated from your female."

"No," Paax said, an amused gleam in his eyes. "Someone blew up my house, stabbed my mate and forced me to challenge the warlord."

"Still, I would do nothing different."

The warlord dismissed the map. "Go. Spend your remaining time with your mate. When you return, we will decide what duties can be delegated to others."

Finished at last, Mylomon raced to the orchard. He was late. Very late. He rehearsed how to explain himself. By the time he arrived, his mate had left.

The blanket and food basket sat abandoned on the grass. The window panel set up as a screen glowed with light. The film was over. He had failed his mate. All the tasks he had that day and he failed the most important one.

He did not believe there was anything he could say to beg her forgiveness but he would try.

When he arrived at their quarters, Daisy rose from

the sofa and went into the sleeping room. Momentarily he was distracted by a rich, heady aroma coming from a pile of boxes on the table.

The door locked behind her.

"Open the door, female."

"No." The voice was muffled but firm.

"Do not make me come in there."

"Oh sure," she said through the closed barrier, "this door you can break down." Breaking down the door was nearly impossible but he could easily phase through it, not that he wanted his mate to see his abnormality.

"I intend to share a meal with you, female," he growled.

The door opened. Daisy stood in what he recognized as her fighting stance with hands on her hips and her feet firmly planted. "My name is Daisy. Not *female*."

This was the moment to apologize. To confess that he lost track of time as he learned to balance his duties and his new responsibilities to his mate. There would be no honor lost in acknowledging the truth. She worked long hours in medical and would work without complaint in the midst of a crisis. She would recognize him as a valuable member of his clan. Indispensable. She would understand.

He found himself unable to express those thoughts. Instead, his attention turned to the green box on the table. Unable to resist the alluring scent, he opened the box.

"What are you doing?" she asked.

CHAPTER NINE

DAISY

DAISY FOUND MYLOMON STANDING OVER THE CARD-board box when she opened the bedroom door.

"Your Earthly possessions have arrived," he said.

She flinched at the turn of phrase. The Relocation Committee shipped her junk. "That's not what that phrase means but I get your meaning. I'll unpack all this junk tomorrow." In the days following her match, when Meridan was still floating in the tank, Daisy had sorted through her stuff. Amazed at how many clothes she'd accumulated, she recycled much but set aside her favorites.

Then she recognized the box. It was not a plain cardboard box but a deep green plastic box with a small clasp to secure the contents. There were some *personal* items she didn't want the Relocation Committee to see, so she packed them herself.

Now Mylomon held the box, giving the flimsy lock a curious look. "This one smells... intriguing."

"No, don't!"

He paused but then snapped off the lock.

Daisy prayed for the floor to open up and swallow her.

Mylomon held up a large, vivid magenta vibrator. Ridges ran down the side. It was the "realistic lifelike alien dominator" and her absolute favorite toy.

She wanted to die. Her skin burned bright red with embarrassment.

"What is this?"

"Nothing." She snatched it out of his hand, clutching it to her chest protectively. Mylomon reached for it but she danced out of the way. "It's personal."

"It smells like your cunt."

And how would he know what that smelled like? Never mind, she didn't want to know.

But she sort of did.

"It's a toy, okay," she said. "Lots of women have them. It's normal."

His attention returned to the box. "There's more. Are these all toys?"

"Yes, okay?" She tried to grabbed the box but he held it aloft. "Now give it back."

The box did not hold a lot of vibrators but he picked them out one by one and inspected. He examined a curved blue rabbit vibe that was great on her clit. He sniffed the thin purple wand, one she didn't really care for. Why did she pack it? It should have been recycled. The whole box should have been recycled.

"What is the purpose of these items?" His tone sounded innocent but a smile tugged up the corner of his mouth.

"You damn well know what they're used for." Self-pleasure was a normal part of human sexuality. She wasn't ashamed, despite how her skin flushed red. Mortified? Yes. Ashamed of her ability to give herself an orgasm? Nope.

"Why do you have so many?" Again with that half-smile.

Big purple jerk.

If that's how Mylomon wanted to play, fine. She'd play.

Daisy planted a hand on one hip. "Sometimes a girl has to experiment until she finds out what she likes."

He lifted another vibrator, this one purple and curved. He sniffed. "And did you like this one?"

"The size and shape is good but the motor is puny. Not enough oomph." Might as well be honest. Mylomon had to have a stash of porn around some place. She'd poke around and then rake him over the coals, interrogating him about what turned him on.

She didn't hate the idea.

He turned his dark eyes to her, his gaze sweeping over her from head to toe. "Which one do you like?"

She tingled at his deep, commanding voice. It sent shivers all over, especially between her thighs. She held out the alien dominator. It was comically large in her hand. She had to be really worked up to get the toy's thick shaft inside her and it sucked down batteries like it was going out of style but it had a deep, thrumming vibration that really hit the spot.

Did it matter that it was modeled on a Mahdfel penis? Would Mylomon comment on that? Would he sense that she liked to pretend that the magenta vibrator belonged to her alien husband? Why was she trembling, waiting for his approval?

"I am larger," Mylomon said with a scoff.

Daisy licked her lips, fighting the urge to glance down at his loose fitting togs. Oh hell, she was only human. She glanced down. His cock made an impressive tent at the front of his trousers.

"Show me," he said.

"What?"

He folded his meaty arms over his chest. "Show me, wife."

She should storm off, enraged and indignant. She should refuse him. Claim he repulsed her. Promise that he'd never touch her. But Mylomon watching her use a vibe on herself?

She didn't hate the idea.

"Okay."

Daisy headed toward the bedroom but he snagged her elbow. "Here," he said, pointing to the sunken sofa.

"Fine, but no touching me."

"I agree to your terms."

She started to unzip the dress but paused. How did she want to do this? Like she just came off shift and needed to work out her tension? Usually she just stripped off her pants and got business done. Or lazy mornings when she woke up from a particularly intense sex dream, desire still coiled tight in her gut and needing release? Or maybe as an angry fuck after a failed date night?

She glanced at Mylomon's shirtless chest.

Yeah. That would work.

He studied her movements intensely. She could do anything and the alien would eat it up.

Wickedness pulled her lips into a grin. She removed her shoes and shimmied out of the dress. The fabric fell to the floor in a whisper. Somewhere in the back of her mind it registered that her husband had never seen her naked before.

"Sometimes I wake up and I'm really horny," she said, arching her back to unclasp her bra. "I just want, no *need*, a nice thick cock in me."

Wearing only a pair of tiny, lace panties, she stood mostly bare before her husband. She pushed down the waistband, noticing how his eyes followed her every movement. Slowly the skimpy lace slid down. She moved to the couch and sat with her knees primly together. "Like this?"

He growled.

Daisy smirked and opened her thighs. "How about this then?"

Another growl, this one approving. He moved in a dark blur and stood before her. The magenta vibrator rested on the cushion next to her.

She took it in her hand and started the motor. "Now every gal is different, but I'll show you what I enjoy." She spread her lower lips and worked the vibe against her clit. On the lowest setting it was a gentle hum. A warm, tingling sensation spread throughout her. She sank further into the cushions, spreading herself wider. The speed increased and she worked the vibe from her clit down to her hot core. She wasn't ready to take the entire vibe, not yet, but she could feel her wetness.

She pushed the bulb shaped head against her entrance and then journeyed back up to her clit. She held the thrumming device against her sensitive nub, letting the sensation wash over her.

"Do you think of anyone?" His deep and rich voice wrapped around her.

"You. I think of you." And she did. She thought about her husband a lot recently. She pushed the vibe in, ready to accept its ribbed girth.

He stood between her thighs, eyes blazing. He reached for the vibe. She flinched away. "I will not touch you," he said as he pushed it in deeper. With his free hand he stroked himself.

He wasn't handsome, not by a long shot. His features were too harsh, too sharp, but she liked his face. It suited him. The way he looked at her, like she was the best thing in creation, was more attractive than a strong jaw or a straight nose.

The rumbling filled her, shaking her core and spreading throughout her body in a haze of joy. Her hands kneaded her breasts, teasing the nipples.

Mylomon took it all in, studying the way she arched her back, the way her thighs quivered and nearly clamped shut as she approached climax. True to his word, he did not touch her but she touched him. Hips bucking, she pushed herself against his hand, letting the vibe sink all the way into her until the point where his hand cupped her pussy.

"I think of you, wife," he said, cock in his hand. He worked his length over her. Daisy couldn't help but stare. She had seen him naked from the back. Had shared a bed with him but she had never seen the equipment he was packing.

He wasn't joking about being bigger than the vibrator.

Damn, she was a lucky girl.

"Do you think about being inside me?" she asked.

His hand pumped along his shaft, circling down to the dark head and back again to the root. "I think how tight you are. How hot. How wet for me," he said with a growl.

Stars, his voice. Sinfully dark as chocolate, it wrapped around her. She wanted to keep feasting until she couldn't move. The growl went straight to her center and sent her over the edge. Her hips lifted off the cushions and her thighs trembled as her climax washed over her.

Mylomon came with a roar, hot seed spraying across her abdomen and breasts. Chest heaving, he stood over her, menacing but not a threat. Not to her. Never to her.

"You are so dirty," she said, panting.

Mylomon reached down and slid the vibrator out. Her juices dripped off the toy. With a satisfied grin he licked it clean.

"I take that back. You're filthy." And she didn't hate it.

MYLOMON

HE FETCHED A CLEANSING CLOTH FOR HIS MATE. SHE did not protest as he swiped the cloth across her stomach and chest. Perhaps his hands lingered too long in the valley between her breasts, perhaps not. She did not protest. She watched him with hooded eyes, a sated expression on her face.

This pleased him beyond measure.

Soon he would claim his mate. He'd bury his cock deep inside her, rather than stroke himself off over her luscious form.

Not that he wouldn't do it again if she asked. His cock stirred at the notion. Patience. He messed up on date night. He would not fail again.

The Relocation Committee had delivered many boxes to their quarters that day but one box in particular had called to him. It was placed on the small table. The enticing aroma pulled him in and he could not resist opening it. Yes, it was a violation of his mate's privacy. Yes, he knew better than to paw through her possessions. Yes, his mate's response could have been far worse but he was bold and took a risk.

And she liked it.

When she turned bright red, a color he now knew was linked to embarrassment, he anticipated her running away. Instead the female responded to his bold words with bold action. How fortunate was he to have such a vibrant female?

"Watch a movie with me," Daisy said.

He settled on the floor, at her knees. Normally he would consider watching a film or movie to be a waste of time. But now with his mate? He'd sit at her feet all day if it pleased her.

She played a twentieth-century animated show about the future with foul-mouth, alcohol guzzling robots and strange aliens, or what the ancient humans imagined the future would be. They were partially correct on the aliens.

Eventually his mate grew tired and she stretched out on the sofa. One hand drifted to the top of his head and lazily stroked his hair. He dared not move a muscle, dared not to breathe, lest he ruin the moment.

He was a fortunate male indeed.

CHAPTER TEN

DAISY

MYLOMON WAS GONE WHEN DAISY WOKE. TYPICAL. She showered quickly, scrubbed off the day-old makeup and dressed for the medical bay. Kalen finally stopped giving her busy work and now gave her genuine work. She was to train the other medical staff in emergency response techniques for humans. The human body was a lot more fragile than a Mahdfel's and required less force on, say, compressions to staunch a bleeding wound. It would be unforgivable if a Mahdfel medic hurt a human mate while trying to save her.

Not that a mate would ever come into harm's way. Daisy knew the Mahdfel bristled at the suggestion that they could, possibly, at some point in the future, maybe fail to protect their mates. The idea was an insult to them, their clan and their honor. Still, shit happened.

Meridan was not in the mess, eating her breakfast. The sisters fell back into a comfortable routine of meeting for breakfast, just as they had on SCLB. Bagels and coffee. The coffee was super important.

Daisy plopped down next to Vox. He immediately grabbed the coffee from her hand and gave the brew a sniff. His brows knitted, unimpressed.

"Why can you not bring me coffee that way I like?" he asked.

"How about you get your own coffee," she replied cheerfully.

"Lazy female."

"Pigheaded male." She took a sip, making a production of it. "So where's Merri?"

"She is preparing for the mission," Vox replied without thinking. He paled. "I was not meant to tell you that."

"What mission, Vox?"

"There is no mission. You misheard me, Mylomon's female."

"What. Mission. Vox." She punctuated each word with a jab of her finger. He growled a warning but his growls didn't scar her. She was married to the scariest monster on the ship. What was Vox compared to Mylomon? "You might as well tell me. You know you can't keep a secret from me."

Vox sighed, shoulders slumping. "Fine. Kalen and Meridan are to go to the planet's surface. I do not know why," he said when she opened her mouth to ask. "I only know that I am piloting them down in thirty minutes."

"Aren't there Suhlik on the planet?" She had a vague recollection of Paax speaking to Mylo about a raid.

"Yes. It will take a very talented pilot to safely reach the surface," he said, chest puffing out with pride.

"So this is a combat situation." Vox nodded. "And they're taking *Merri*? The baby nurse?" And not her, the trained combat nurse with battlefield experience.

Screw that noise. She was tired of being ignored. "I'm getting on that shuttle, Vox, and you're helping me."

"I cannot. I was not supposed to share that information with you."

Daisy patted him consoling on the shoulder. "Don't worry about it. I won't tell if you don't."

"What am I not telling?" A puzzled expression settled on his face.

Poor, sweet Vox. Daisy should be ashamed of the way she took advantage of him. "You're going to get me a set of flex-armor. Step to it, fly boy. Hurry, hurry, hurry."

She wasn't proud of herself. After abusing Vox's clearance into the armory, she bullied her way onto the shuttle and used Kalen's reluctance to upset her sister as leverage. Not her best moment. Honestly, though, what were her options? They were taking Meridan? An obstetrics nurse? Into a combat area? When Daisy was literally a combat nurse with field experience? She didn't flinch at explosions and kept her cool under pressure. But bring the baby nurse who doesn't like loud noises, sure. That made sense.

So she got her happy butt on that shuttle. As the party approached the planet, Daisy realized she only wanted on the mission to spite Mylomon. Yes, it was childish but she still smarted from last night. If his work was more important than her, than her work was more important than his commands for her to remain on the ship.

Yeah, the reasoning was off but it made sense that morning when she suited up in the white and red flex-armor.

Behind her in the party's formation, Kalen spoke to Meridan. She didn't want to eavesdrop, honestly. Was it even eavesdropping when they were two feet away?

This was a dead planet. Ruins of building littered the canyon they marched through, covered in years, perhaps decades of vegetation growth. Once there had been a civilization of sentient people here. Then the Suhlik came and did what the Suhlik do best: they killed everyone.

Not one person was left alive on the planet. It could have happened a year ago or a hundred years ago. It was impossible to tell. But Daisy knew that she walked through the skeletal remains of a world and Earth had nearly shared the same fate.

This would have been Earth if not for the Mahdfel. She was glad when they finally exited the graveyard of the past and approached the Suhlik research facility.

Perched on the side of the canyon walls, they hiked up a staircase carved into the rock.

The warlord and the rest of the clan waited at the top. Paax only raised an eyebrow at Daisy, as if not surprised to see her at all, only exhausted at the thought of the inevitable fight between her and Mylo.

As if on cue, a demon filled the doorway. Dark, darker than a deep wine, Mylomon absorbed the light. His horns curved out menacingly. He looked like a monster. Her monster.

When he spoke, his words were cold, dispassionate and completely at odds with his barely controlled demeanor. "Female, you were ordered to remain on the *Judgment*."

Daisy stepped back at his words but steeled herself. She planted her feet firmly, hands on her hips. "I can be useful here."

"You can be injured here. This is no place for an unskilled female."

Daisy's nostrils flared with stubborn resolve. She didn't want to fight in public but she refused to back down now. "I am not unskilled!"

"I cannot guarantee your safety. This planet is swarming with Suhlik."

"So you want me to stay in our quarters like a prisoner? Why don't you cover me in bubble wrap?"

"I would if it would stop you from disobeying my orders. Return to the *Judgment* at once."

Daisy lifted her chin. "No."

"Female, do not defy me on this."

"No. I'm staying."

With a growl, Mylomon scooped up Daisy, tossing her over his shoulder like she weighed nothing.

"Put me down, you monster!" Daisy's fists pounded against his back uselessly.

"You will obey your husband, female." One arm curled up, holding her in place. The other secured her legs to stop her from kicking.

"Let me go!"

Mylomon turned to the warlord. "Sir, I will return this one to the *Judgment*."

Paax nodded. The dark warrior took off at a fast clip, nimbly navigating the steep steps.

"I'll never forgive you," she shouted, fists continuing to pummel his rock-hard shoulders and back.

"But you will live. Why do I care if I have your forgiveness?"

"Don't you dare try to act like you care about me!" More pummeling.

His large hand swatted her bottom. The sharp stinging broke through her rage fueled rant and went straight to her core. "Do not presume to tell me what I care about, female."

"You spanked me!"

"And I'll do it again if you do not hold your tongue."

The firm authority in his deep and soothing voice ignited a warmth in her stomach and between her thighs. She refused to be turned on by his barbaric display. He spanked her for disobedience? Who even does that?

The better question to ask herself, why did it get her so hot?

"You wouldn't dare." Why did she egg him on?

The smack landed solidly on her ass. The flex-armor absorbed most of the impact but she felt the compression and the sting. She squeezed her thighs together in excitement. What was wrong with her?

Mylomon stomped up the ramp of a shuttle. It was not the medical shuttle she arrived on but a smaller, stealthier model.

He deposited her in a chair. A thick arm planted on either side of her and he leaned down, his nose a hair's breadth away from hers. "Let us understand each other perfectly clear. You are my wife. You may not care for me but I *do* care for your safety and wellbeing. I will do everything in my power to protect you, even if that makes me your enemy and you say hurtful things. I do not care one iota about your duties or where you think you have to go. When you blunder into a corridor full of Suhlik, I will do anything to protect my mate. Is that clear?"

Daisy fought the urge to lower her eyes in submission. He wanted her to look away. He wanted her to give in. Well, screw that garbage. She held his gaze, battling for dominance.

She opened her mouth to say her peace. An alarm beeped, tearing his attention away.

MYLOMON

Could one more thing go wrong? The clan did not meet their objectives on the planet surface. Not only was the Suhlik research facility empty of anyone they could interrogate for access to the second location, they discovered a foundling. A Terran foundling. A female child, no more than a handful of years, shrank back from the warriors. Every question met with a shrill scream.

Mylomon could not begin to fathom what it meant that the Suhlik were taking Terran children, female children, and conducting vile experiments on them. More worrisome was that Suhlik had abandoned the child.

The Suhlik abandoned nothing. It was a trap. The entire thing was a set up: tracing the traitor's signal, the research facility in the valley, and even the surprisingly weak firefight to gain access to the research facility was a trap. And now the alarm confirmed that he failed to protect his mate.

Upset with him, she blundered her way into danger. If he was not so furious he would laugh at the misfortune. Nothing in his life was easy. He had to fight for every scrap and now he had to fight for their lives.

"What's going on?" Daisy asked, following him to the cockpit.

Mylomon sat in the pilot's seat, flipping toggles

and reading the report. "A corrosive gas is flooding the canyon. We leave now."

Now was too late but he didn't want to tell his mate that. The engines needed time to engage. Ship systems came to life too slowly for his taste. If the corrosive gas surrounded the ship, the engines would flood and they would never leave the ground.

Daisy strapped herself into the co-pilot seat, face serious and determined. "I'm not sorry I came," she said.

Mylomon could help it, he smiled. What a female. She had fire in her blood. His cock strained against his armor. "Now is not the time to argue," he muttered. The corrosive gas surrounded the shuttle in a dense, green fog. Escape was now or never.

The shuttle lifted off the ground. It hovered several feet in the air. As he applied the thrusters to lift the shuttle above the gas cloud, the loud whine and screeching of metal filled the cabin.

"That's so not good," Daisy whispered, hands clutching the chair armrests.

Not good. Not the worst thing, either.

A more skilled pilot might have been able to break free of the miasma filling the canyon. Mylomon's skills laid elsewhere. Too bad the gas didn't need to be assassinated. The engine shuttered to a stop and gave up the fight to maintain elevation. The ship landed on the ground with a heavy thunk, the entire structure shaking and rattling the bones of its occupants.

His fingers moved above the control panel. "I have alerted the warlord about our situation."

"My sister?"

He read the reply. "It appears they were able to leave safely." The medic and his mate probably did not lose precious seconds needed to escape being distracted by an argument and they had a skilled pilot.

"What now?" his mate asked.

Mylomon gave her helmet-free head a reassuring stroke. "We wait. The shuttle is able to filter the air."

"If it can't take off in this crude, how can it filter the air?"

He shrugged. "I'm not an engineer." He never really wondered how the mechanics worked. They just did.

"I guess we have time to argue," she said.

"I guess we do."

DAISY

THE SUHLIK USED GAS ATTACKS DURING THE INVASION. Daisy remembered the frantic scrambling as her father strapped on the masks over her and Meridan before securing his own. To poison the very air was so... She couldn't find the right word. Petty? Vindictive? Final.

Final was good. The Suhlik weren't interested in negotiations. They were conquerors. They stripped Earth of its resources, slaughtered and enslaved the people and took the very air out of their lungs.

Daisy wasn't doing herself any favors lingering on the past. Her family survived. Mostly. Her mother died protecting Meridan from a Suhlik scout who spotted the pair while gathering water.

Focus, she scolded herself. Stay in the present.

Monitors displayed various angles around the shuttle. Each screen was filled with a dense green fog. "How long will this last?" she asked.

"Depends on atmospheric conditions. If there is a layer of warm air above the canyon, we will be here for some time."

"That's a cold air inversion, right?"

Mylomon nodded, eyebrows raised.

"I paid attention in science class," she said.

He said nothing but the gleam in his eye said he didn't believe her.

Gah. Big purple jerk. Like she couldn't be good at science. She was a nurse, for crying out loud. She had to be good at biology. That was a science. Or maybe he just didn't believe she was good at anything. Talking to Mylomon was so frustrating and it didn't have to be that way.

He was unbelievable with his little speech about protecting her for her own good, even if that made her hate him.

She didn't hate him. The opposite, really.

"Explain," she said. "What did you mean by a corridor full of Suhlik? What are you telling me?"

He turned his back to her, inspecting the door and the seals.

She stalked over to him. "Don't you dare ignore me again. That's what got us into this mess."

He turned to her, eyes blazing. "Do you think I could ever ignore you? When you are everything I have ever desired? What I do not deserve? How could I ignore such perfection when my touch would taint it?"

She swallowed. Perfection? Sweet but misguided. "You talked about protecting your mate from a corridor of Suhlik. Did you know?" They had only just met in the service tunnels minutes before.

His gaze held hers but he said nothing. Daisy's tongue ran across her lower lip. "Did you know," she prompted.

He nodded and looked away. "I... scented you at the ball. I was unsure how to approach so I elected to wait."

"But then the attack."

"Yes. The attack. I followed you, strictly to ensure your safety."

"And you didn't say anything all those hours we were locked in that cold room?" Quite frankly, if a hot, buff warrior told her that she was his mate and he would personally guard her while the base was attacked... Well, it put a different spin on how they met.

"I feared saying the wrong thing, of making you hate me." His eyes roved the shuttle's interior, looking anywhere but at her.

Was he *shy*? Her big, scary assassin was *shy*?

"Mylo," she said, stepping closer to him. Her hand rested on his chest. She wished there was not a layer of armor between them. She wanted to touch his skin, to feel the warmth of him.

Another alarm sounded.

Mylomon pulled away and turned his attention to the control panel. "I was wrong. Apparently the shuttle is unable to filter the air. We must flee."

He barked out orders. She was to restore her helmet and use the suit's air filtration. He grabbed a knapsack of supplies, stuffing one bag inside a slightly larger bag. She grabbed the medical field kit and added it to the pack.

"Are you ready?" he asked.

"Yes." Daisy mentally prepared herself to run when the ramp opened. Run where, she couldn't say.

As if reading her mind, Mylomon said, "There is a cave system not far from here. I could not locate the entrance but I located where the wall is thinnest. It should be above the gas layer. Hold on to me. Do not let go. Not for a second. Do you understand?"

His words made no sense. The thinnest part of a wall? Did he plan to knock through stone?

"Do you understand?" he repeated.

She nodded. "Sure. Don't let go."

He slung the pack over one shoulder and wrapped

an arm around her waist. Then he shimmered out of focus. A warm, fuzzy sensation spread over her and she realized the entire world went out of focus.

Then Mylomon walked through the shuttle wall.

CHAPTER ELEVEN

MYLOMON

NOTHING HAD EVER BEEN SO IMPORTANT AS THAT moment and nothing was as precious as his trusting mate in his arms.

"Holy shit," his mate said in that endearingly vulgar way of hers. "What the hell was that!"

"Shh," he murmured, stroking her back. He needed to concentrate. Teleporting himself was trivial. He'd done it sleeping, once. Teleporting two was tricky, especially when he carried his most treasured possession in his arms. "Questions later."

"Right, right."

Outside the shuttle, Mylomon surveyed the valley. The green gas created a thick fog he could not see out of. He hated to move blind but there was no choice. Exposed, the suits' environmental supports would not last long. He needed to move. Now.

Through was easy. Moving side to side even easier. To move down, all he had to do was concentrate on being less solid. Up was a challenge. Up was limited in range and drained him.

Running on memory and the map projected on the inside of his helmet, Mylo reached *up*.

He landed solidly on top of boulder. Daisy whimpered but did not complain. She held on tightly. The next move as lateral. He moved from point to point, landing on ledges with the barest of toeholds. He pulled himself up and when he couldn't climb, he teleported. Slowly he worked his way up and over until he reached the last obstacle: a sheer vertical cliff. His destination was ten feet directly overhead.

He was more skilled at teleporting through barriers, past guards and sentries and flickered just past the edge of a knife. He was not built for teleporting long distances or carrying a passenger.

There was no option. His mate needed him. He would not fail.

Drawing on his reserves, Mylomon gathered his focus and reach up. His being vibrated and stretched, carrying Daisy along for the journey. He couldn't make it in one leap. Halfway up, he quickly refocused, slipping back a bit, and leapt again.

Mid-leap, he changed direction and went sideways, through the stone cliff face.

Chest heaving, he set his mate's feet on the solid ground. His arms were slow to release her and she was just as slow to step away. Her grip remained firm.

"We have arrived, female," he said, leaning down to nuzzle the top of her head and wishing the helmets were not in the way.

"What the hell was that!"

DAISY

THE INTERIOR OF THE CAVE WAS COMPLETELY DARK. The embedded lights in her helmet adjusted to provide illumination.

She leaned a hand against the stone wall, unbelievably finding it solid. Or herself solid. Whatever. Her knees wanted to buckle and the rest of her wanted desperately to collapse to the floor. She moved to lift the visor on the helmet.

"Wait. Testing the air quality," Mylomon said. He held up a hand and then motioned that it was safe.

Daisy gulped the stale, cold air of the cavern. Wherever they were, it was closed off from the outside. Or above the canyon. The sour smell of sulphur clung to her armor. The gas transformed into a sticky film upon contact.

Mylomon pulled her in for a crushing embrace. The flex-armor absorbed much but she could still feel the intensity as he poured in what he could not say with words. "I do not care what horrible words you say to me. I do not care if you hate me. You are mine and I will not lose you."

She returned the embrace, wishing the armor wasn't between them. "I don't hate you."

He pulled back and examined a seam at her shoulder. "I have to get you out of this armor."

She couldn't fight the smile spreading on her face. "I know it was a dramatic rescue and all, which is pretty hot, but maybe buy me dinner first, hero."

"The seal is compromised. You cannot let the residue touch your skin."

Ah. Not sexy but necessary. A gas that could ground a shuttle and ruin life support was no joke. She moved to undo the clasps holding the armor together.

"Let me," Mylomon said. "I will start at the top and work my way down. Gloves and boots will be last. Do not touch anything."

"What about your armor? Shouldn't you get out of it, too?"

"Mine is more durable than yours. The seals are not compromised." He removed her helmet and placed it gently on the ground. Next came off the shoulder and chest plate. A smile played on his lips. "I am not so easy to get undressed. I required dinner."

"Was that a joke?"

His typical serious expression replaced the playful smile. "If you cannot tell, then no."

Daisy rolled her eyes. Her big, scary warrior was sensitive. He didn't like to be teased, which made her want to tease him all the more. Instead, Daisy made the choice to be an adult and said, "It smells awful."

"We will not be able to salvage your amour. We will leave it here."

"And yours? It's coated in that stuff. What if I bump into you in the dark?"

He looked down at the growing pile of discarded armor. "If you were Mahdfel I would tell you to watch where you are going, but I know humans have poor night vision. I will remove my armor as well."

"How kind of you," she said sarcastically. He raised an eyebrow at her tone. "Oh, come on, like you didn't know I was going to make you leave that stinky armor behind. You reek. I reek. Everything stinks."

Mylomon slipped off her gloves and, finally, the boots. She was left wearing a long sleeve black top, tight fitting black leggings and a slipper sock designed for exercise with a durable lining on the sole. The slippers were a shade better than being barefoot. Barely. They could protect her feet from scrapes and uneven terrain but they weren't quite up to the challenge of hiking into the unknown.

Daisy shivered, rubbing her hands along her arms. "Are you cold?"

"A little. I'll warm up once we get moving."

Mylomon divested himself of his armor. Daisy

tried not to stare. He was built, after all. And he was her husband. She was allowed to appreciate his physical form. He probably ogled her, too. Not that she ever caught him at it. If she did, she'd probably snap at him for checking her out. So Daisy was a big ol' hypocrite.

Mylomon frown as he removed the satchel of supplies from the outer bag. "You are displeased."

"Do you ever check out my ass?" The blush that overcame her burned fiercely. Thank the stars the cave was dark.

"Every opportunity."

Her chuckle was free and easy. Mylo delivered the line with such convincing seriousness but she knew, just knew, that he teased her.

She liked this side of him. Too bad they had to get stranded on a dead planet to find that out.

CHAPTER TWELVE

MYLOMON

HE LED HIS MATE THROUGH THE DARK CAVERNS. Fresh, gas free air meant the caves had an exit above the canyon. He could smell water in the distance. He had a vague idea of which direction was up. Other than that, he let his heightened senses guide them through the dark.

If this worried his mate, she said nothing. She used a flashlight in one hand to illuminate the floor and held his hand with the other, allowing him to lead her. He enjoyed it. Not because she needed him, but because they worked together. Even if she did fill the time with meaningless prattle about Terran films and questions about his clan. She had not yet asked about his teleporting, the ability that saved them from the corrosive gas. He knew though, that she was circling the topic from above like a bird of prey. She was waiting for her moment, the perfect moment when he would be most amiable to discussing it honestly, and she would strike.

She had the mind of a tactician. He admired it.

He admired several things about her. She caught him by surprise when she asked if he ever observed her posterior. He had. It was pleasingly round and the way it swayed when she walked was fascinating. He would not lie about that. There were several physical attributes about her that he admired, like how her golden hair caught the light. Or the perfect curve of her hips. And the way she planted her hand on one hip when she was upset. Or her smile and the way it pierced the darkness in his heart.

Daisy smiled frequently. She did not hide her joy but too often her smiles were for others, not for him. He wanted those smiles. He did not want to share. So many things in this universe had never been for him.

But Daisy was for him. Against all odds, against all probability, she was for him.

And he did not want to share.

Of all her admirable qualities, she was patient. She did not hate him when she had every reason to. He had been a neglectful mate.

His mind kept returning to the way she handled herself as the shuttle crashed. She strapped herself in and calmly followed his instructions. She did not panic. She did not wail and blubber. As he brought them above the fog, she gasped once in surprise. No questioning. No demands for explanations that would slow down their escape. Even now, her chattering was a way to maintain her calm. She was tougher than he expected.

Perhaps this was what she had been trying to tell him for the last month but he was too stubborn to listen.

"Hello? Earth to Mylo? Did you hear me?"

"Apologies, female. I am listening for water."

"What about fire? I'm freezing over here."

The night would be cold. They had discovered no kindling thus far. "We will share the reflective blanket for body heat." The blanket in question was currently wrapped around his mate.

"You make it sound so romantic."

"You are teasing me."

"Yes, I am, big guy. I like the way your nose scrunches up when you think."

"My nose does not scrunch. It is a noble and proud nose."

"It does and it's *adorable*."

His mate smiled. He heard it in her voice.

"So, are you going to talk about it?"

Ah. She lowered his guard and seized her opportunity. "Very well."

"You're not even going to pretend not to know?"

"You want to ask about my teleportation. What else could you want to talk about?" He did not wish to discuss what the Suhlik had done to him but it seemed easier in the dark. The dark shielded him from pitiful looks. He was not a creature to be pitied.

"Okay, I'll start. What the hell, Mylo? You can teleport! That is so freaking cool. How? Since when? Why didn't you tell me?"

Her reaction was not what he expected. "I can. Since I was a child. You know I was a foundling. The Suhlik engineered this ability into me. They made me into an abomination. And that is why I did not tell you."

She squeezed his hand. Again, not the reaction he expected.

"So is it more a Nightcrawler ability or do you just phase through stuff like Kitty Pride?"

"Those words mean nothing to me."

"Can you move yourself at a distance or are you limited to moving through objects?"

"Both."

Another squeeze, followed by a swing. "That is so *cool*."

"You do not understand, female. The Suhlik stole me as an infant. They slaughtered my family. They changed my genetic code to be their instrument. This ability separates me from the clan. It makes me different. An abomination."

"Oh, sweetie." She stopped, tugging on his hand to pull him in. She rested her head against his chest. "If you had ever shown up to date night with me, you'd know that I freaking love superhero movies. Love 'em. And maybe I've always had a thing for big, strong alien men because they remind me of Superman. I don't know. We're not analyzing me right now. What I do know is that having a mutant power has always been my deepest wish. Well, you know, along with being rich, and beautiful, and dating the boy from third period math and my mom being alive, a super power was it."

"I am not a mutant."

"You just said the Suhlik changed your genetic code. That sound like a mutation to me, sweetie."

He searched her words and tone for distaste or worse, pity. "You are not revolted?"

"Because of the teleport thing? There are lots of things about you that make me want to pull my hair out but teleportation ain't one."

His chest rumbled. He was unsure if he was pleased or frustrated. Vexing female.

"You said you can hear water. Will there be enough to bathe? We stink."

"We are close," he said.

They continued their journey in the darkness. He reviewed their conversation. He could not find a single hint of pity from his mate. She accepted his greatest flaw without hesitation. It excited her.

He would never understand how the female mind worked.

DAISY

Tired and cold, Daisy did not notice when Mylomon stopped moving. Not until she walked into the back of him. "What is it?" she asked. More Suhlik? Wild animals? A four-star hotel and luxury resort?

Please be a four-star hotel.

"We'll make camp here."

Daisy swung the flashlight wide, examining their location. It was a cavern with a curved roof. The walls glimmered in the light. In the center was a pool of water. Steam curled off the surface. "Is that a hot spring?"

"Yes. This place has many such features." It wasn't a four-star hotel and luxury resort but it was close enough.

"Is it safe?"

He crouched at the edge and scanned it. "Safe to drink when cool."

"Safe enough to have a bath?" Every part of her smelled like rotten eggs. Sulfur. Ugh.

"Yes, but we do not have a fire to dry yourself."

Right. No fire equaled shivering wet in the dark cave. No thank you. "Tomorrow?"

"Tomorrow we will gather fuel for a fire, then you may bathe." Mylomon opened the supply bag and gave her a ration bar and a bottle of water.

"I can't believe you totally turned down skinny dipping with me." She took a small bite. She was hungry enough to shove the entire bland bar into her mouth but she paced herself.

"We have no fire. You will be cold and your immune system compromised. I will not allow you to become sick."

"You can't forbid me from catching a cold, Mylo."

"I can and will."

She snorted but did not argue. She washed down the rest of the tasteless bar and finished off the water. A yawn escaped.

"Rest, female. Tomorrow we hunt and forage for supplies."

Daisy shivered. The steam from the hot springs was warm near the pool but on the edges of the grotto, the air was damp and chilled. "You don't think we'll be resc—retrieved?" Not rescued. There was nothing to be rescued from.

"Only tomorrow knows but a wise warrior prepares."

So that was a solid nope. No rescue. They were on their own, at least for the next while.

"I guess the clan is busy chasing down whoever let off the gas."

His eyes narrowed. "I'm sure the warlord has many objectives."

But her husband wasn't sharing them with her. Fine. Be that way. Daisy said, "There's only one blanket."

"We'll share."

"On the ground?"

"You said you lived in the wilderness during in the war."

"A cabin in the woods. We had a mattress." She and Meridan had shared a bed, more for the body heat than the lack of additional beds. The winters got cold in the mountains.

Mylomon sat down, back against the stone wall and folded his legs lotus style. He patted his lap. "Come. We will do this as we did before."

"You mean when we were locked in a morgue? Charming. Let's repeat that." Though sarcasm laced her tone, she couldn't help but lick her lips.

Mylomon raised an eyebrow. "Sleep, female."

"Just sleep?" What was getting into her? It was more a question of what *wasn't* getting into her. She was tired, cold, hungry, stinky and seriously thinking about climbing all over her gorgeous purple husband. She should straddle his lap, grab him by the horns and pull his mouth to hers.

Daisy shook her head to clear her thoughts. Calm. Control that libido. There'd be plenty of opportunity for horn grabbing in the future, preferably with a bed, two blankets, heat and food. "Just sleep," she said.

She climbed into his lap. She jostled for a moment, trying to get comfortable.

"Female, are you doing that on purpose?" Mylomon sucked in his breath, his body going stiff.

A lot of him going stiff.

A smile ghosted across her lips. Good to know her husband wasn't as immune to her as he pretended. "I'm trying to get comfortable. See. I stopped moving."

"You'll be the death of me," he muttered.

Daisy bit back the sarcastic reply of "yeah, but what a way to go" or "you love it." She was feeling playful and Mylomon didn't play. He was super serious all the time. She rested her head against his chest. The thud-thud of his heart pounded a soothing rhythm.

Her breathing slowed, matching his. His arms settled around her and the blanket enveloped them. Warmth soaked into every muscle.

"This is a lot nicer than last time," she said.

"We have a blanket now."

"That's not what I meant. I like you better this time."

The muscles in his abdomen tensed. "You don't mean that."

"Mylo, my dear husband, you can walk through walls but you can't read minds. Don't tell me what I think." She tried to keep her voice sweet. She *tried*. She wasn't looking for a fight. Not really.

"No one likes me," he said.

Exhaustion made a pretty strong argument to keep her mouth shut and go to sleep. Correct him in the morning. Ignore the self-loathing. Go. To. Sleep.

She couldn't ignore a person in pain.

Daisy shifted, tilting her head back to look at him. Shadows completely hid her husband's face but she had an idea that he frowned. Glowered. Tried to intimidate her to leave it and not talk about it.

What a bunch of garbage. You don't say something

like "no one likes me" and then not want to talk about it.

She should have taken that psych class in school.

"Your clan likes you."

"I frighten them. They tolerate me."

Right. Assassin. Mylomon didn't play by the same rules as the rest of the clan. "The warlord likes you."

"Perhaps. I believe Paax respects me but he is resentful about past decisions and punishes me with a heavy workload."

"Is that why you're never home?" He said nothing but his arms gave a gentle squeeze. "What about Mercy?" It was hard to imagine the very pregnant Mercy disliking anyone. She always had a smile on her face.

"Paax's female hates me."

"What? Why?" The possessive need to defend Mylomon stirred in her, which was ridiculous. Mylomon was a full grown male. He was huge. He did not need a mouthy little woman to defend him.

"Actions I took under orders from the previous warlord."

The pointed comments Mercy made, which Daisy overheard, about stabbing and blowing up houses made sense. Order from the previous warlord, Omas. Right. No one in the clan voluntarily talked about the disgraced warlord. Everyone agreed that the clan thrived under Paax and that seemed to be enough to satisfy the urge to gossip.

"Did Omas like you?"

He stroked her hair, his touch so light as to almost not be perceived. Then, "I do not know. I liked him. Once."

"That sounds like there's a story involved."

With barely a touch, he somehow worked her hair free from the braid and his fingers ran through her hair. He seemed content to stroke her hair.

Daisy elbowed him in the stomach. "That means I want you to tell me about it."

"Hmm. Oh. Your hair is not one solid color. There is variation in the strands. It is very pretty."

"I'm surprised you can see anything in the dark."

"Mahdfel vision is stronger than Terran."

"Don't change the subject. Story time, bub."

"Omas was the warrior who found me."

"When you—"

"Yes."

He grew silent. Daisy didn't press. He might be

thinking about all the things the Suhlik had subjected him to when he was a child and unable to defend himself. Or he may have been remembering the warrior who carried him to freedom, like a proper superhero. Or he might have been thinking about how his butt was getting numb on the stone floor. She had no way of knowing.

"He was not always insane" Mylomon said at length. "Once he was a honorable warrior and a good warlord. He was my friend."

A friend whose defeat and death he helped to orchestrate. Yup. Totally needed those psych classes.

"Many people care for you," he said, squeezing her in an embrace again. "It is impossible not to like you."

"Glad you think so but people find me annoying."

He tensed again. "Who would dare say that to you? Speak their names and I will avenge you."

"Chill. I was exaggerating." She patted his chest for reassurance. It was like striking stone.

"You care for many people. Meridan," he said. Then, after a pause, "Vox."

"Merri is my best friend, you know. After our mom died, she tried so hard to take care of me. Still does. Sometimes she doesn't treat me like I'm an adult but that's okay. I know she's overbearing because she loves me. I do the same to her."

His chest rumbled in agreement.

"She's so serious, you know. If I left her alone, she'd just work and sleep. Work and sleep. So I make her be social. I drag her out to dinner, to films and whatnot. She says I'm immature but she needs to lighten up. Live a little." She yawned, covering her mouth with her hand.

"And Vox?"

"Are you jealous?"

"Perhaps. You spend much of your free time with the male."

Daisy remembered back to Vox's concerns about being alone with another male's mate. "He's careful. We only hang out in public areas. No closed doors. Never alone. Besides," another yawn, "he's only there because you're not." Given a choice, she'd rather spend time with her husband.

"I ordered him to keep you company."

Daisy sat up straight. "Did you?"

Nearly blind in the dark, she felt him nod. "Truly."

Huh.

All those evenings she spent alone, he thought of

her. Gave her companionship, even though it was not his. She misread the situation entirely. Mylomon was busy. He held an important position in the clan. Was that not what Vox tried to tell her but she was too stubborn to listen? Her husband *wanted* to spend time with her but couldn't, so he sent her friend.

"That's sweet," she said. "Thank you."

His arms pulled her back in and settled around her. "Tell me about this Date Night that I missed. What would we do?"

"It would be a lot like this, actually. Talking. Getting to know each other. But with more, you know, smooching." Hopefully. Stars, she wanted smooching.

"Interesting."

"Interesting so let's try it?"

"No," he said, voice firm. "We have no fire. It is too cold for nakedness."

"Wow, naked smooching. That's a big leap of logic there, sweetie. I mean, it sounds fantastic. I'm totally on board but how about we just start with a good night kiss?" She tilted her face upwards, ever hopeful.

"Agreed."

His lips brushed against hers, soft and hesitant. It was sweet but not what she craved.

Daisy surged upwards, hands planted on his shoulders and claimed his mouth with her own. Her tongue licked the seam of his lips and pushed, opening him to her. Hot and wet, their tongues entwined. A shiver of delight coursed down her. She nipped at his lower lip and pulled away. "Good night, love," she said, voice husky.

His arms stiffened.

Shit. She'd never said the word love before and yet it slipped out. Surprise. Well, it was a hell of a good kiss. What should she do? Assess. Adapt. Make a joke. Play it off like it was no big thing, like it wasn't their first kiss and she didn't accidently confess her love.

Daisy patted him on the chest. "Schedule in some more smooching time for tomorrow, sweetie. I liked it. We need more of it."

His muscles relaxed. "We have a full agenda but I'll see what I can do. Good night, female."

CHAPTER THIRTEEN

DAISY

THE CAVE SLOWLY GREW LIGHTER. OUTSIDE THE SKY was a soft, foggy white. Mist hung in the canyon below. When patches in the mist cleared, they saw the noxious green fog still remained. They were going to be stuck here for a while longer.

Daisy washed her hands and face in the freezing cold water of the grotto. Mylo handed her a ration bar. Bland and dense, she chewed her way through the bar.

"We need to conserve the rations," he said.

"Right, because they're so tasty. We might scarf them down."

"Because they are nutritionally balanced and we do not know what kind of sustenance we will find here."

"Food is food," Daisy said, mimicking his words in a gruff tone.

"All food does not have the correct vitamins and minerals our bodies require."

"Are we going hunting?" Her interested perked. She shoved the remaining portion of the bar in her mouth and got to her feet. The last time she was on Earth, she went hunting with her father. They came back empty handed but the time together was worth it. Hunting with Mylo could be the bonding opportunity they needed. He liked knives. They could talk about knives while he stabbed the local wildlife.

"I am hunting. You will remain here."

Her hand went to her hip. Mylomon planted his feet on the ground. Battled positions assumed.

"I don't think so, bub."

"What is a bub?"

"Oh, no. Don't distract me by being all cute because you don't know idioms or slang. That only works on me once."

He grinned, just the smallest flash of white teeth against his dark complexion.

"I can hunt," she said.

"Not here. This is an unknown environment. You have no idea of the animals on this planet."

"And you do?"

"I am Mahdfel." He folded his arms over his chest. He had made up his mind and the conversation was over.

Right, right. Daisy rolled her eyes. He was a superior alien warrior. What a garbage reason if ever she heard one. "I'll stick to small prey. Bunnies are bunnies everywhere."

"Do you know why this is a dead planet?"

This sounded like a trick question. "Kalen said that the Suhlik invaded here long ago and killed the original inhabitants." Which would have happened to Earth if the Mahdfel hadn't shown up to save day.

Mylomon nodded. "And the Suhlik use chemical weapons. Weapons that alter the environment. Weapons that mutate." He emphasized the last word, mutate. At least he listened to her little speech about being pro-mutant. "Bunnies here are not necessarily bunnies."

"Mutant bunnies," she said.

"Yes. Please remain here while I scout and hunt."

"And if you don't find killer mutant bunnies?"

"Then I will give you my rifle and sit by the fire, enjoying the life of a lazy male."

"We don't exactly have a fire, either." Daisy motioned to the empty ring of stone on the cave floor.

Mylomon nodded and handed her his knife. "Gather wood. Do not go far. If you find..."

"Bunnies?" The knife had a good weight in her hand. Substantial but not too heavy to wear her out if she used it. The blade had a thick spine and a gut hook on the tip. The finger grooves on the handle were a bit large for her grip but the bolster was large enough to protect her hand if she slipped. This was a knife designed for hunting, not combat. She tucked it into the waistband on her pants.

"Anything, return here. Run. Do not let this knife make you confident."

"I understand. What about foraging for food?"

He gestured broadly to himself. "I explained my purpose, female."

"Right. What if I just happen to stumble across a nice looking bush full of berries or some tasty roots?"

"Scan them with your wrist unit to see if they are edible."

"Basic government issued model, remember?"

Daisy thumped the nearly invisible band on her wrist. The model had basic functionality for communications and none of the fancy features boasted at the higher end. "Normally I'm on the base, er, ship, and it doesn't matter."

"You *should* be on the ship now."

"Don't start with me." She rolled her eyes and shook her head slightly.

"Bring the edible back and I will scan them. Do not test them yourself."

She nodded. She wasn't completely green in the field. She knew better than to stick alien plants in her mouth and hope for the best.

"Swear to me." His gaze grew in intensity, peering right through to her core of her being.

"Yes. Of course."

He grabbed her chin and lifted her face toward his. He leaned down and pressed his forehead to hers. "It is my instinct to forbid you from leaving the cave but I will not waste my breath. You will not listen. Be careful, my mate. You are my heart."

The big purple goof.

Daisy stretched up on her tiptoes and landed a quick peck on his lips.

Mylomon drew back, surprised.

Look at the big, scary assassin, surprised by a kiss. Daisy couldn't help but grin. "I am stubborn, not stupid. I'll be careful."

* * *

THE FLAW WITH GATHERING WOOD FOR THE FIRE WAS the distinct lack of wood.

Well above the canyon, the mouth of the cave opened up onto a tundra. A flat, grassy, treeless tundra. Moss covered boulders dotted the plain. Mountains in the far distance were a dark smudge against the milky sky.

Scenic.

She was learning how to communicate with her husband. Last night they made good progress. Pseudo-date night. She smiled warmly at the memory. Daisy used words to express herself. Mylomon was all about the action, like a real superhero. Her superhero.

Daisy had it bad. Her attraction to Mylomon had grown into affection. Love, even. Was it even possible to love someone when there was so much left to learn about each other?

Maybe the discovery was the exciting part.

Hmm.

The ground had a faint squishy quality. Her steps squelched as she stalked toward a cluster of tall grass. Grass could burn. Not well and not for long but it would be good kindling.

Animal scat remained her best bet for fuel. Good thing she had gloves and soap. She kept an eye to ground, looking for droppings.

She passed low, scrub like bush with vivid berries that looked all the world like blueberries. Careful not to prick her fingers, she plucked a handful. Then she hacked off a few branches for fuel.

As she reached the tall grass she realized it was not grass but cattails. Or a near-alien cattail-like plants. Close enough. There was a cob at the end and it lined the banks of a small stream. The stalk and root of Earth cattails were edible. The cob, when dried, could burn. Cattails even had a starch that, when dried, acted very much like wheat flour.

During the wilderness years of the invasion, the Vargas family did not have fields of wheat but they had all the cattails Daisy and Meridan could carry. She spent so many hours soaking, pulverizing and separating out the starch from the root, she could do it in her sleep. Had on occasion.

Daisy plucked off the cob of the older growth and stuffed it in the fuel bag. Once satisfied, she moved to the younger stalks. Grasping firmly at the base, she pulled it up by the roots.

The stubborn plant didn't want to give. Daisy worked in the knife, to loosen the roots. The root system seemed to be more complex than the Earth variety. Hopefully they were edible. Mylo would be able to tell her with a scan of his comm unit. Roasted cattails. They might be bland but they'd be hot and hot food sounded really good.

Another pull and she ripped the root from the mud. She teetered back, foot slipping and fell on her butt in the cold mud.

Grumpy but determined, she pried up four more plants, roots and all. There. That should be enough to munch on if edible. If not, she hadn't wasted too much time. A muddy butt was a reasonable price to pay for a vegetable side dish. They might even taste good. Wouldn't that be something?

Daisy washed her hands in the water, frowning at

the mud under her fingernails. Mylo had soap waiting in the cave. She sat on a moss covered boulder near the water's edge and loaded up her harvest into a bag.

Ready for the return journey, the boulder underneath her shifted, then heaved upwards with a roar.

Daisy tumbled to the ground and scrambled backwards, her hands flying up to cover her hands.

The boulder unfurled itself.

No, that wasn't right.

The giant, moss covered armadillo-bear creature unrolled itself and stood on it hind legs. It towered over her.

Panic flooded through Daisy. Her feet wanted to run. Really, really fast but she suspected not fast enough. She forced herself to be calm. Assess. Adapt. The armadillo-bear looked *sleepy*. It had been napping in the sun when Daisy parked her butt on it's back. Bad idea. She'd been so focused on mutant bunnies she forgot about the mutant boulders. At least the creature seemed to be as surprised by her as she was of it.

The knife lay in the mud, just out of reach. Daisy carefully scooted to one side. The armadillo-bear huffed at her. Slowly she stood up, holding out her hands and arms to make herself appear as big as possible. That worked on Earth bears so it was worth a shot on alien armadillo-bears. Right?

Right?

Well, she didn't have any better ideas so she stood there, knife in one hand, arms extended as wide as possible, praying for the bear to not be feeling a bit snacky after his interrupted nap.

She took a step back, foot sinking into the mud.

The armadillo-bear moved forward.

Daisy waved her knife, shouting as loud as possible. "Stay back! The male I got this from will be super pissed if I gunk it up with alien bear guts!"

The creature took another step forward.

Daisy moved back but lost her footing, twisting her ankle as she fell down into the water. The bear stood over her, it's odd flat head cocked to one side. The knife slashed wildly, glancing across it's snout.

It roared back in surprise more than pain. A heavy hand smacked Daisy down. The knife slashed again, the blade glancing uselessly off the armadillo-bear's rock-like hide.

Seriously, what was this thing?

A dark shadow inserted itself between her and the enraged bear, growling. A plasma bolt from the rifle hit the creature in the paw. Squealing in surprise, it ran off.

Mylomon stood above her, back to her, shoulders heaving, as he watched the creature retreat.

Finally, his breathing slowed and he turned to Daisy. "Are you injured?"

"I'm fine." He offered a hand to help her stand. On her feet, she winced. "I rolled my ankle, I think."

With a huff, he lifted her and cradled her to his chest. They said nothing until they reached the cave.

CHAPTER FOURTEEN

DAISY

MYLOMON SET HER DOWN ON THE CAVE FLOOR, careful not to jostle her ankle. "I'm fine," she said, pushing him away when he examined her.

"Female, be quiet." Strong fingers prodded at the swollen joint.

"It's a sprain," she said. "I am a nurse."

"Terrans are fragile. What if you tore a ligament?"

"I'd be in a lot more pain." He gave her a doubting look. "Honestly. It only hurts when I put weight on it."

"So don't put weight on it."

Daisy nodded. "You see me sitting on my butt?

This is me being a good patient. Normally I'd ice it and elevate."

He moved the supply bag under her foot and arranged it just so, huffing when satisfied. "Are you comfortable, female?"

"A fire would be nice. Maybe a soak in the hot springs."

Mylomon set about his work of building a fire. He brought over the already skinned and butchered carcass of a small animal, presumably an alien bunny, and set it to roasting. He followed Daisy's instructions for preparing the cattails and put the roots on a flat rock next to the fire to roast. If he did not see the value in cooking plants, he didn't mention it. She risked her life getting those cattails. She was damn well going to eat them.

"Can I have a bath while the food cooks?" she asked.

He undressed first. Daisy tried her hardest not to leer but she was only human. Unclothed, he helped her undress. His hands skimmed her form, barely touching and she tingled in response. She gave the shirt a sniff before tossing it in the water. It smelled strongly of muddy water and could use with a good scrubbing. With the combined warmth of the fire and the hot springs, the cave was downright cozy. With the last garment off, he lifted her and carried her to the edge of the pool.

He climbed into the water first, then lowered her in. "Good?"

She sighed with pleasure as the hot water enveloped her, soaking into her sore muscles. "Yeah, good," she said.

He took out the cleansing bottle and began to lather up her back and shoulders.

"You don't have to do that."

"I will care for my wife as I see fit," he said. His voice, deep and delicious, wrapped around her, as warm as the water and twice as satisfying.

"I love your voice," Daisy said, closing her eyes and leaning back. His hands worked out the tension in her shoulders then moved lower.

He paused momentarily before continuing. "What else do you love?"

"Making a list?"

"Perhaps."

Perhaps. His favorite word. "I like lots of things," she said.

"Like? I asked what you loved."

Facing away from her alien husband, Daisy did not hide her grin. With his senses, he could probably smell it or something. "You nervous and require validation?"

"Mates should praise each other." He worked the lather into her hair. His strong fingers massaged her scalp and Daisy's eyes rolled into the back of her head. So good.

"So you are fishing for compliments."

"There are many things I like about you," he said, his voice growing thick. "I like your laugh. I like that you are not afraid to laugh at me. I like the fire in your blood. I like this." He delivered a playful swat on her bottom.

Daisy yelped but did not move away.

He gently pushed her on the shoulder to dunk under the water.

"I'm not afraid of you," she said, sputtering from the dunk.

"I know. I like that, too." Rinsed to his satisfaction, he turned her around to work on her front. He paid careful attention to lathering her chest, his hands cupping and squeezing her breasts more than necessary.

She didn't hate it.

Actually, she liked it. A lot.

He scrubbed down her thighs and legs, dunking underwater to tenderly massage her feet. His hands worked across her abdomen, drifting down. Excitement coiled in her stomach. She wanted his touch. Craved it. When his hand finally cupped her mound, she placed a hand on his chest. "My turn," she said.

"I am not done with you, female."

"Oh, I agree, but I want my fun exploring you and all those muscles."

Grumbling, he handed her the bottle of cleanser. With a wicked smile, she lathered up her hands and set about exploring the hard lines and contours of her husband.

He was hard. All over. Solid. His skin was warm with just the slightest amount of give. Definitely not fat. Maybe a cuddle layer. Something so a girl didn't hurt herself against him.

She worked up a thick lather in his hair. Short and shorn on the sides, it did not take much. Then she ran her sudsy hands along the wild curves of his horns. Mylomon moaned so loudly she jerked back in surprise. "Did I?"

"Apologies. They are sensitive."

Gingerly she returned to them, paying closer attention. The texture was like velveteen stretched over something hard with a hint of pliability, like cartilage. "You like that?" she asked, knowing full well he did.

"Female—"

One hand remained on a horn and the other wrapped around his cock, hard and ready. His eyes flew open in surprise. She stroked him in both places, moving her hands at the same rate, loving the way his body trembled. Her strong, scary monster helpless at the touch of one little woman.

Mylomon was objectively hot. No question about it. Driving him wild with her touch? So much hotter. "Husband," she whispered, "I want you."

Moving faster than she could perceive, he scooped her up and set her at the edge of the pool. He opened her thighs and leaned in, examining her. "You are the finest thing I've ever seen. I wonder how you will taste, wife." He parted her lower lips and licked along her sensitive slit. Daisy tilted back her head and moaned.

His tongue rasped against her, working her clit and darting into her core. Her hips bucked and she ached to be filled, to be claimed. Finally, a finger prodded at her entrance and pushed in. His fangs lightly scraped her sensitive button and she gasped when he sucked. He worked his hand in and out, in and out, and her legs kicked in the water.

Mylomon was terrifying but she knew he would never, ever hurt her. She'd never felt as safe as she did in that moment with her husband feasting between her thighs and her body quaking with ecstasy.

Her released was building. She wouldn't be able to fight it off for much longer. "Mylo, I need you."

He growled, the vibrations edging her closer. Another finger pushed in. Then a third. They angled together in a come hither motion, hitting the right spot. Daisy fell apart and came together again, shouting her husband's name. His tongue and hand remained in place as her orgasm subsided.

With a satisfied rumbled, he climbed onto the edge and pulled her to him. "Best thing I've ever tasted."

She tapped his chest lightly and chuckled. "You are filthy."

"You indicated you liked that."

"Oh, very much so. Now," she said, rolling onto her back and displaying herself. "Are you going to claim you mate, warrior?"

His expression closed down, all emotion drained away. "I will not."

What. The. Hell.

MYLOMON

"Why haven't you claimed me? Don't you want me?" She sat upright, arms wrapped protectively around her luscious form. The hurt in his mate's voice was obvious enough for even an unobservant male like himself to hear.

She believed he didn't want her.

Guilt stabbed at him. Nothing was farther from the truth.

He cupped her face with a hand and she leaned in, eye closed. "I want you, female." More than anything. More than the entirety of his being.

"Then don't stop," she said. "I want you, too."

His mouth captured hers, soft lips yielding to his demands. The sweetness of her cunt lingered on his tongue. He could take her again, let her flavor explode over his tongue once more, but he would not claim her. Not here. Not like this.

Daisy pulled away, panting. Her pupils were wide and her skin flushed. She gazed at him expectantly, then frowned when he remained still. "What's wrong?"

"Not like this," he said.

"Why not? I'm all warm and fuzzy from the hot springs and," she blushed, "you know. And you're excited." She waved a hand toward his obvious erection.

"You deserve better."

"Fine." Her words said she was not upset but a crease between her eyebrows marred her face. Aggressively she pulled on her shirt, tugging down the fabric like it insulted her. Like he insulted her. She took out the comb and worked it through her golden locks.

"You are upset."

Daisy rolled her eyes. Her face was so expressive. Mylomon enjoyed watching her thoughts and emotions flicker across the canvas of her face. Normally. Now stormy thoughts clouded her otherwise open and sunny disposition. "Of course I'm upset, Mylo. I'm horny and naked and my gorgeous husband doesn't want to make love because he has self-esteem issues."

Her reached for her hand, pulling her back to him. "You deserve better than a dirt floor in a cold cave. You deserve a fine meal, wine, flowers, and music. As much as I want you now, as much as my desire aches in me, I will wait until I can give you those things."

"They're just things, Mylo," she said, her voice soft. "I don't need them."

"But I need to give them to you." Couldn't she see that? He was unworthy in so many ways. The fact that she was eager to bind herself to an abomination was beyond belief. The least he could do was respect her enough to not rut on the bare ground like an animal.

Daisy closed her eyes and pressed her brow to his. "Okay," she said at length. "We wait until you're ready."

He pulled her into an embrace. She buried her face into his chest. "You think I'm gorgeous?" he asked.

"Stop fishing for compliments. You know you are."

"I question your eyesight but know that I, too, think you are gorgeous."

"I knew you were a sweetie pie." She yawned.

"The food is finished. Eat. You will need your strength tomorrow."

CHAPTER FIFTEEN

MYLOMON

H E WOKE WITH HIS COCK ROCK HARD, NESTLED BE-tween the checks of Daisy's ass. With her back pressed against his chest, he completely forgot about his moral stance on claiming his mate the correct way. The situation was both torturous and perfect. He could roll her over onto her stomach and sink into her warm, hot core. She pleaded with him to do just that last night. His big mouth talked him out of claiming his perfectly formed mate.

He moaned with frustration, lifting his hips ever so slightly. Nothing about their situation had changed and waking up with an erection wasn't leave to disrespect his female.

Daisy deserved to be claimed the proper way. Or as proper a way as he could manage and he could manage a hell of a lot more than the cold floor of a dark cave on a forsaken planet.

He was disappointed at his own sense of right and wrong.

Daisy stretched, rubbing against him. Gritting his teeth, he rolled away and climbed to his feet. There was no point in torturing himself when there was work to be done.

"Good morning, sweetie," she said with a yawn. Then she caught sight of his massive erection. "Oh."

"It is nothing," he grumbled. If he ignored it, the throbbing would diminish.

"I'd hardly call that nothing. Come here." She reached for him and licked her lips. She couldn't be serious.

"Female—"

"Daisy," she said. "If I'm putting your dick in my mouth, you can call me by my name."

He swallowed. Hard. She was so bold. "That is not necessary."

"I'll be the judge of that. As I recall, you took care of me last night and I kind of ignored you like a bitch."

He growled. He did not like to hear her speak about herself in derogatory terms.

"Right, right," she said. "Forget I said that but I do want to give you something."

She knelt before of him, hands on his hips. The dark head of his cock rested against her plump lips. The tip glistened with pre-cum. Her little pink tongue darted out and licked up the moisture. His knees nearly buckled from the sensation. She hummed happily. "You taste really nice, husband. Why haven't I tried this before?" One hand cupped his balls and the other gripped the base of his member. Her tongued dragged up and down the sensitive underside.

"We have been busy," he gritted out.

"Seems like this is something we should always make time for," she said, looking up at him through the fringe of her messy golden hair. "Don't you think?"

"I think you're the most beautiful thing I've ever seen."

With a smile, she took him into her mouth. Wet, searing heat surrounded him. She opened wide and took him deep, swallowing and breathing through her nose. Mylomon growled in satisfaction, pumping into her. His length dragged across her tongue and lips and pushed back in again. There was nothing as sweet and good as his wife.

He came with a roar, hands holding her in place, gushing into her. She drank every last drop. Finished, she pulled away and licked her lips. A satisfied smile lingered.

Mylomon lifted his wife to her feet. "You are my heart, wife." His arms wrapped around her and he pulled her in for a kiss. Salty flavors lingered on her tongue. Himself, he realized with a start. Underneath that was her giving sweetness. He drank her in.

"You big softie," Daisy said, patting him on the chest. She repeated that motion often, a casual display of affection. He enjoyed it and growled to let her know. Her eyes widened. "What was that for?"

"That was for my wife."

She shook her head with a laugh. "Aliens."

"Come, eat. I will fashion a crutch for your ankle."

DAISY

"WE ARE BEING WATCHED," MYLOMON SAID. HE STOOD at the entrance to the cave. Daisy squeezed around him to get a better view. She scanned the empty horizon and saw nothing but the little hairs on the back of her neck stood up.

"Yup. Something's going down," she said.

Mylomon went out shortly after dawn and returned an hour later with a sizable tree branch. Where he managed to find a tree, she didn't know. He peeled off the rough bark and rounded the end with a knife and carved it down to the right size to fit in her hand.

She leaned on the walking stick, letting it take the weight off her ankle. Today the ankle in question was swollen and tender but she could walk. Well, hobble.

Something metallic gleamed, catching her attention. "There really is someone out there. Is it our clan?"

"Doubtful."

Verbose as always.

Still, there was sunlight and clear skies. The weather had changed overnight. The cold, grey misery that kept the gas trapped below in the canyon had cleared out. "How's it looking down in the canyon?"

"Gone," her husband replied.

"So we can go home? Get in our shuttle and leave? Have a real bath and food." And make love in their bed like he promised.

Gah. Daisy shook her head to clear her thoughts. Wound tight, her mind kept circling back to Mylomon: his perfectly sculpted chest, broad shoulders, and thick cock—he had stuffed his entire length down her mouth and she would never believe could take it all, but she did. How would it feel to have that inside her aching pussy?

She was so doing it again. As often as possible, preferably.

"Life Support was damaged. We cannot take the craft back to the *Judgment.*"

"So we wait for rescue." Another gleam. "Seriously, what is that?"

"A Suhlik scout," he said.

"Do they want us to notice them?"

"Yes. They wish to draw us out." The communication unit on his wrist beeped.

Excitement flared in Daisy. "Is that the warlord? How long have we been able to talk to the ship?"

"Only recently and text only. Voice is not supported at this distance." He read the message, a frown on his face. Not good news, then.

"What does it say?"

"I am to leave you and pursue the Suhlik."

"No!" She didn't even have to think about it. Beyond being by herself on a planet full of mutant bunnies, armadillo-bears and now Suhlik, she wanted to stay with Mylomon. "I'm going with you."

"You cannot." A frown crossed his face as he gave her a critical look.

"Why? Because I'm Terran? Or because I'm a woman?" She squared her shoulders, preparing for a fight. If that big purple idiot thought he could treat her like a dainty little thing made of spun glass, he had another thing coming.

"Because you can barely stand. How will you hike a great distance? Climb? Run?"

Her shoulders sagged. "Don't leave me alone. What if they want to separate us?" Why would the Suhlik even care about her? It was best he didn't look too closely at her argument.

He studied her and rubbed his chin. "Fine," he said. She rushed forward and wrapped her arms around his waist. "But only because I know that even if I command you to stay, you will follow me."

"See, we're learning so much about each other, sweetie. Now you know I'm stubborn and I know you can't resist my puppy-dog eyes."

* * *

FOR-FUCKING-EVER LATER.

Actually, only an hour later but it felt like forever with her ankle. It whinged with every step on an uneven surface and considering how they were hiking across the tundra, that was nearly every step. Mylomon had been right, as much as it pained her to admit. She should have stayed in the cave and waited for the clan to send a shuttle. Probably Vox. With Meridan because Daisy was absolutely certain that her sister would insist on being part of the rescue party.

Daisy wasn't the only stubborn one in the family, after all.

Still, she didn't like the idea of being separated. It made her nervous. The safest spot on this planet was right next to her big, scary monster. Well, in his arms was the safest. Next to him was pretty darn secure.

"You are smiling, female."

"What? This? It's nothing. I'm just practicing my expression of placid tranquility when you go on about how you were right about my ankle and staying behind in the cave."

He stopped in his tracks. "Are you in pain? Do you require me to carry you?"

Actually... Being carried in his arms sounded really, really good. Excitement coiled in her belly and warmth spread throughout her. Too good. Better to not be all snuggled up in Mylo's massive arms. Even if it was the safest, snuggliest spot on the planet. "Not yet. I've got a little more steam in me."

They journeyed in silence until Mylomon crouched down. Daisy followed. "What is it?"

He pointed to the distance. "A disabled Suhlik fighter. It must have crashed when the clan cleared the planet." And the misty, cloudy weather had kept it hidden.

"Is it occupied?" She shifted her weight, favoring her ankle.

Mylomon noticed. "Stay here."

He took out his knife and crouched into a sprinting position. In a blur, he was gone.

Daisy couldn't help herself. She stood up, leaning on the walking stick. Her husband pulled a Suhlik male out of the cockpit of the fighter. The fight was either over that fast, or it had never even started. She limped over.

The Suhlik was in rough shape. A fresh wound in his shoulder bled freely. Mylomon had the knife to the male's throat and his other hand pressing into wound. The Suhlik barred his teeth and snapped.

She would never get use to the Suhlik's contradictory appearance. They had a sublime, golden beauty Earth culture considered ethereal. Angelic. Paired with two rows of razor sharp teeth, two sets of oddly blinking eyelids and retractable claws, their entire visage changed to terrifying when aggressive. And they were always aggressive.

"Female," Mylomon snarled. "I told you to stay back."

"And I told you I don't listen."

He grunted but returned his attention to the Suhlik. "My friend, we need to have a conversation."

The Suhlik spat a string of curses at Mylomon. Her translator was slow to render but the gist was mostly "freak" and "atrocity." Outrage boiled inside her. If anyone was the atrocity, it was the Suhlik, whose people had committed genuine atrocities on her planet, this planet and countless other.

Without hesitation, Daisy picked up a fair sized rock from the ground and pelted it at the male. "How dare you, after what your people did to my man!"

Another hiss, this one directed at her. "Control your female, freak."

Daisy threw another rock, this one landing directly between its eyes.

"Female, cease!" Mylomon snapped.

Her skinned chilled at his harsh tone. "I'm sorry," she said in a quiet voice.

Mylomon's eyes flashed. Perhaps he regretted his sharp tone. It was hard for her to say. He returned his attention to the Suhlik under his knife.

"Let me explain how this is going to work, friend. You *will* give me the access codes. You *will* tell me the correct code and not the decoy code. I *can* tell when you are lying. Like right now. You're snarling and snapping at me but I literally have my finger on your pulse. Can you feel it?" Mylomon paused. His hand sank into the male's shoulder. More than just into the wound. Into the shoulder, like up to his wrist, much like how he moved through walls. Flesh was another solid object, after all.

As fascinated as she was, she felt as if she would pass out. She focused on her breathing to stay conscious. She could do this. She'd been elbow deep in bloody soldier's chests before. This was no different. Mostly.

"I will give you nothing, freak."

Mylomon's hand sank in farther. The Suhlik passed out.

"What did you do?" Daisy asked. She crouched down next to the unconscious male, searching for a pulse. There, weak but alive. Mylomon pulled her back.

"I applied pressure to an artery. He will wake soon."

"How did you know to do that?" As soon as the question left her mouth, she wanted to take it back. It was a useless question. She knew how he knew. He was an assassin. Murder was his business. "Forget I mentioned it," she muttered as she scooted away.

"I am the tool the Suhlik made me," he said.

The Suhlik stirred.

"Good of you to join us," Mylomon said. His voice, normally deep and soothing turned dark. Threatening. Daisy shivered. "Now, about those codes."

The Suhlik spat at him. Mylomon shook his head as if disappointed. "I forgot to mention what would happen if you failed to cooperate." The knife moved downward, too quick to follow and there was the sound of flesh being torn and then the shriek of the Suhlik.

Mylomon held up the severed finger. "I find cooperation to be so helpful. You've got nine more opportunities to be cooperative or you can continue to be a dick. What are the access codes?"

The Suhlik opened his mouth wide and lunged, snapping like he wanted to bite Mylomon's face.

Mylomon pinned his back to the hull of the ship with one hand. Correction, not pinned exactly. The palm of his hand sank into the male and vanished. "Shall we try again?"

The Suhlik's eyes grew wide and he coughed.

"What did you do?" Daisy asked.

"I gave him his finger back. His lung seemed a good place to hold it." The male started to shake and tremble. "Don't worry. It won't kill you. It just hurts like the nine hells."

Daisy could not turn away while her husband worked. He was a butcher. He carved information out of the Suhlik. It was not graceful or clean. It was not even the task he was designed to do. He was the wrong tool for the job, a hammer trying to drive in a screw. It was monstrous.

This was him. This was the work he did for the good of his clan. His clan had every reason to shy away from him. He worked in shadows and did not follow their rules. He tortured. He killed. He was a monster.

He was her monster.

Daisy knew with absolute certainty that Mylomon would never, ever harm her. He would tear apart the universe to reach her.

Satisfied he extracted the correct information, Mylomon worked the knife across the Sulik's throat. In the end he brought swift, merciful death.

He spun toward Daisy. A blank, stoic expression settled over his face but she could see the uncertainty in his eyes. He feared her rejection and she had every reason to turn away in disgust. Her husband was not a proud, noble Mahdfel warrior. He was something else. Something darker.

She wanted a big, strong alien warrior. She got that and so much more. Big, strong, dangerous, dark and completely devoted to her. She knew that in her bones. Now that she saw him for who he was, finally, she wasn't going to let him go. "When we met... Why were you on the moon?" she asked.

"I cannot say."

"I think you better say."

He cleaned the blade on the grass before sheathing it. "I was on a mission. Am still on a mission. There is a traitor."

"Go on."

"Someone has been transmitting information to the Suhlik."

"What kind of information?"

"Locations of our children."

Daisy let the information work its way through her brain. There was traitor selling information to the Suhlik. The shield at SCLB fell suspiciously fast. The Suhlik were always raiding and snatching children, like what had happened to Mylomon. "Someone is selling Mahdfel sons to the Suhlik?"

He nodded. "Two, I believe. One must be Terran. I came very close to finding the traitor but—"

"The raid happened," Daisy said with a nod.

"I found you."

"What?"

"At the Harvest Ball. I was in the same room as the traitor, hunting, but I could not locate the signal with so many people. He was hiding in plain sight."

"The Purloined Letter," she said.

"What?"

"It's an old story about hiding a letter with other letters so it blends in. Camouflage."

"Yes. The traitor used the event to hide from me. Then you walked by in that dress and your scent hit me and there was nothing else for me."

It should not have been sexy the way he stared at her with such intensity. He had another man's blood on his hands. There was a dead body less than two feet from them and all Daisy could think about was how she needed her husband to kiss her.

Mylomon broke eye contact. "We traced the signal to this planet, where we found a research facility in the canyon. But there was a second signal."

"Also on this planet?"

He pointed to the mountains in the distance. "There. We are going to infiltrate that base."

"We?"

A smile flickered across his face. "I know if I command you to stay, you will follow. And now we have transportation." He motioned to the fighter jet.

"Can you fly that thing?"

"Yes."

CHAPTER SIXTEEN

DAISY

THE FIGHTER BARELY HAD ROOM FOR THE TWO OF them. The narrow craft was a two-seater but it was not designed for Mylomon's bulk. He jammed himself into the cockpit. Daisy squeezed into the backseat.

Under protest and with a few false starts, he got the bird into the air.

Two hours into the flight and the mountains seemed no closer. Her legs and butt were numb from sitting. She shifted in the seat but it was not designed for comfort.

An alarm sounded. Daisy examined the monitors

but the written Suhlik language looked like gibberish to her. "I think that's trouble."

"They know we are here," he said.

Another alarm, this one higher pitched. "That sounds bad."

"Have they locked target on us?"

"Maybe. I don't know. There's a bunch of green lines and red dots on this screen."

"That's bad," he confirmed. Fantastic. "Hold on."

The fighter banked hard. Blasts peppered the belly of the ship, rattling the shields but holding.

"Shield percentage," he barked.

Daisy desperately searched the monitors for something that looked like a shield or a shield symbol. "I have no idea. I can't read Suhlik." Two new, massive red dots joined the monitor. "We got incoming. Big."

"More fighters."

"I thought the clan cleared this planet."

"What is that Terran insect? You kill one and there's a hundred to take its place?"

"Cockroaches. Just focus on flying. I think this is the gun." She flipped open the cage surrounding a joystick. It better be the guns.

A new image of the fighter chasing them appeared

on the monitor. Targeting systems came online. Daisy had no real training at flying or dogfighting but she'd spent many hours with Vox playing video games. She lined up the targeting system, watching for the symbol to turn green and fired.

She beamed with pride as a missile slammed into the fighter. The shielding absorbed the hit but she was onto something. Suhlik fighter design was not that different from the simulated Mahdfel crafts. Thank the stars Vox wasted so much time gaming.

The next hit got through the shield and the fighter fell back. Unfortunately, it was joined by two more. They overwhelmed her. Daisy fired randomly, lucky to hit anything.

Their shielding failed and the engine was hit. The fighter pointed to the ground and Mylomon struggled to keep the nose up.

"Are we crashing?"

"The engine is out. This is an unscheduled landing. Strap yourself in."

Amazingly the Suhlik fighter jets turned back. Why would they give up pursuit now? Her thoughts were cut short.

The fighter slammed into the ground, belly scraping

across the tundra. Metal tore with a high pitched screech as the plane gouged into the land. Safety harness engaged, Daisy jostled and her teeth rattled. She could feel her brain bouncing inside her skull.

Finally, the fighter jet came to stop.

Metal ticking as it cooled, Mylomon unstrapped himself before helping her out of the wreckage. A laceration on his forehead bled mightily. She moved to clean his wound with a first aid kit. He caught her by the wrist. "No time for that now."

"I thought you said you could fly this thing."

"Fly, yes. Land, no."

Daisy couldn't help but smirk at his unintentional quote from a favorite movie of hers. "I can't believe this is the second ship you've crashed."

Mylomon grumbled a warning, delicate little flower that he was. "We have far to go before we rest, female."

MYLOMON

HE WORRIED ABOUT THE RAIN. HE WORRIED ABOUT HIS mate in the rain. He worried about his mate walking on her injured ankle in the rain on muddy, uncertain ground.

Many worries crowded his mind. If he were on the *Judgment*, he would go to the training arena and spar with a mech until his mind cleared. Or he would sharpen his blades until his mind reached clarity as precise as those honed edges.

He could do nothing here. Just walk and worry.

Daisy had witnessed everything. Every dark secret he wanted to keep from her, this wretched planet dragged out of him. But she did not turn away in revulsion...

That was interesting. What was it she was always going on about? Communication. Learning how to talk to each other.

Words had never been his friend. Action was direct and could not be misconstrued.

He had taken many dark actions in the past. Some at the orders from others. All for the good of the clan. He was stillness and silence; the knife in the dark. He had remorse for those dark, necessary actions, but not regret. The knife in the dark flew against the Mahdfel understanding on honor but it saved time and lives.

His mate did not turn away from him as he

extracted information from the Suhlik male. She understood the brutality of necessity.

Strange. He rubbed at his chest, a familiar tingling sensation just below the surface of his skin. If he had a tattoo, he knew, it would be glowing now with strong emotion.

She had told him time and again that she did not mind his abnormality. That he was not an abomination in her eyes. She accepted him as he was. He had not believed any of it. Until now.

Perhaps communication was not what he lacked. He needed to listen.

They walked until the sun hovered over the horizon. He kept an easy pace but he knew Daisy struggled. She refused to let him carry her, even though she weighed next to nothing. He could sprint all day with her clinging to his back and not break a sweat.

He sat his mate down with the remaining ration bar and bottle of water. He set about making a fire. The campsite was next to a cluster of stone. Not idle but not completely exposed.

Fire blazing, he sat on the ground next to his mate. He reached for her hands to inspect for damage.

"I'm fine," she protested.

"Your ankle is injured and you refuse to acknowledge it. What other injuries are you withholding, female?"

DAISY

"MY NAME IS DAISY," SHE SAID, ATTEMPTING TO TUG away her hand. "I'm too tired for this nonsense, Mylo."

His grip remained firm, his thumb brushing across the sensitive flesh of her wrist. "I know your name."

"Then use it." Big purple idiot.

"I am not worthy to even speak the name of someone as good and pure as you." He released her hand, scooting away. His gaze fell away.

Daisy's heart lurched. There was so much self-loathing to unpack in his confession. Years of rejection and otherness had warped his sense of self-worth. She wished there was a way to fix it, to repair his ego and restore his perceived value with words. The best she could do was be honest and explain herself. Mylomon wasn't a mind reader, after all. He could walk through walls. Stars, he walked through walls *with her* but he still couldn't read minds.

"When you don't say my name, I feel unwanted," she said.

Fast, faster than humanly possible, he rushed forward and captured her face in both his hands. His eyes burned with a frightening intensity. His grip firm but not crushing, Daisy was unable to turn her head and look away. "You know that is not true."

"Do I? You're never around. I go to bed by myself. I wake up alone. Feels like you're avoiding me."

"I know a female such as yourself could never love an abomination. I hoped that if you could not love me, I could give you someone you did love." His hands dropped and he looked away. "I authorized the test for Meridan."

Daisy leaned back and exhaled slowly. There were a few ways she could respond. "You are not as the stars made you. You are as the Suhlik made you but I love you. Not despite. Not because. I love you." And every word would be true. Or, "Prove it. Claim me. Right now. Make me your mate."

What she actually said: "You did *what* with my sister!"

CHAPTER SEVENTEEN

DAISY

CONFLICTED DIDN'T BEGIN TO COVER HER EMOtions.

Daisy clambered over the mossy rocks, heading toward a stream. She might as well forage for some almost-cattails. Now that she knew what the armadillo-bears looked like, she avoided the slumbering animals. Time out of the campsite gave her time to unpacked all that Mylomon confessed.

He had authorized Meridan's test.

On one hand, Mylomon understood that being separated from her sister upset Daisy, so he gave her back her sister. But on the other hand, giving a person as a gift? Who even does that?

He was sensitive to her emotional needs, which was a good thing, but his actions... Intentions mattered, right? He wanted Daisy to be happy and if happiness meant being in the same clan as her sister, then he did what was necessary.

Mylomon had already made his speech about doing what was necessary for the good of the clan, even if it made him unpopular. So he understood that his gift was wonderful and terrible? Awful in both senses of the word. And what if Meridan hadn't been matched to Kalen? Mylomon took a huge risk based on what? Nothing. He guessed.

She and Mylomon were a 98.5 five percent match, which was the legal minimum for a match. She heard stories of women who accepted their match with a 98.4 percent risk. Close enough for horseshoes and hand grenades, right? She also knew plenty of women who wept with relief at the same, non-legally binding number.

She was getting distracted. Daisy plunged the knife into the mud and dug up the newer stalks. New growth had a crunch, mild edible stalk and roots that could be roasted like potatoes. She took her frustration out in stabbing at the the ground and yanking the cattail stalks.

If Meridan found out, she'd never forgive the invasion of her privacy, even if her legally mandated marriage turned out happy in the end. She hated people making decisions for her.

Mylomon gave Daisy her sister, but he also gave her a secret to keep from her sister.

Crunching grass underfoot made Daisy pause. She scanned the area and did not see the obvious source of noise. Probably an armadillo-bear having a snack. She focused her attention back to digging.

What was Mylomon playing at when he took such a gamble with Meridan and Kalen? Mylomon's actions told her that he considered her happiness important, more important than a clan member, more important than the self-actualization of another person. You don't wrap up another living being with a bow and give them as a gift. People don't do that. And what did it say about Daisy that it secretly thrilled her?

The cool metal of a gun barrel pressed into the side

of her head. "Drop the knife, female," a voice hissed. The slight lag in rendering told her it was a Suhlik warrior hissing instructions.

Daisy stopped her digging and held up empty hands.

"It took you long enough to wander away. On your feet, ape." The gun prodded her to stand. Water sloshed into her completely inappropriate-for-the-wilderness slippers.

Daisy glanced quickly at her captor and then down to the ground, like a meek little human. Assess. Just one Suhlik and quiet enough to sneak up on her. If he wanted her dead, she'd be dead.

Resources? A knife left in the mud. A husband stewing in his own grumpy mood in a cave. And armadillo-bears. Lots of slumbering armadillo-bears.

"Move," the Suhlik ordered. No gun prods this time. The weapon hung lax at his side.

Typical Suhlik arrogance—expecting her to just go without a fight.

Daisy broke into a run, heading for the closest hibernating animal. She made it four steps before a prick in her lower back made the world blur.

Well, what a load of garbage.

MYLOMON

HIS MATE FAILED TO RETURN BY SUNSET. VEXING female. What point did she intent to prove with this tantrum? She only endangered herself in the dark. Her ankle was already stressed from traveling all day. If she stumbled in the dark, her delicate Terran bones could break. Or she could be lost. Or have fallen in a sinkhole.

A dozen scenarios flickered through his mind, none of them good and all ending in disaster.

Mylomon put out the fire and grabbed the flashlight. Time to retrieve his female.

Daisy's tracks were obvious. In her anger, she failed to obfuscate her footprints. He followed the trail to the stream.

His own anger and frustration grew with every step. Her rage at him made no sense. He'd acted in good faith for her. Then this foolish tantrum. Childishness. What did she hope to gain? To tell him she was upset? Fine. He got the message. Her insistence on wandering in the dark did nothing but endanger herself.

Females.

Did every male have these complaints or was his female just particularly difficult?

She had fire in her blood, that much he could not deny. And did he not want a female with intensity? How could he complain if the fire in her blood matched the venom in her tongue? He was being an ungrateful male. What was the Terran words she slung at him?

A big purple idiot.

A familiar tingling sensation spread over his chest as her recalled with approval the way she set her hands on her hips. Her fighting stance. And she could be sweet.

Incredibly sweet.

Hmm.

He needed to find her. Apologize. Convince her to let him lick her cunt again. Yes, that was a good plan.

Daisy's trailed ended at the water's edge.

Mylomon grew cold at the signs of the obvious struggle. Cattails pulled by the root were scattered on the ground. Heavy footsteps crushed the grass and marred the mud. He found her knife tossed to the side a few feet away.

Two sets of footprints. The new set was difficult to

find in the dark but find it he did. A stealthy approach. Then an ambush on his mate, who was busy pulling cattails up by the root.

He followed the struggle as the unknown assailant dragged Daisy. Her feet kicked at the ground, leaving him a trail. Then the struggle ceased.

Mylomon growled, crouching down and touching the dead grass. They injured his mate. Or incapacitated her. Perhaps both.

The trail continued, now the uneven gait of one person carrying another. After half an hour, the trail ended in a clearing. The flattened grass and scorched earth told him a shuttle had landed here.

Mylomon knew who took his mate and where they would go.

His captors hoped to lure him to their lair. The Suhlik wanted their foundling back.

CHAPTER EIGHTEEN

DAISY

THE BONE CHILLING COLD WOKE HER.

Daisy rolled onto her back, the spongy floor giving under her. White walls. White ceiling. White floors. Fuzzy memories of the Suhlik solder grabbing her surfaced. Panic seized her throat but she fought through it with long, deep breaths.

Assess.

Adapt.

Survival was non-negotiable. Her story did not end here. She knew how her story ended: at home, in her bed, old and surrounded by her half-dozen sons, each one she busted to the seams with pride over, much to their embarrassment, and Mylomon holding her hand.

She wanted that, more than anything, to grow old with her husband. They'd had a rough start as they learned how to communicate with each other, but they would pull through. Daisy knew it. She wouldn't settle for less and no dumb space lizard would to keep her from her man. Male. Whatever.

Daisy sat up slowly. Her head throbbed and nausea sat in her gut.

Assess.

She was naked. Of course. Don't all alien abductions start that way? Knock the woman out, strip her down and then experiment in the most violating way?

Panic tried to return but Daisy refused to let panic cloud her thinking. The Suhlik wanted her to feel vulnerable. This was part of their mind games.

And she was alive to play a game with; that was worth something. If the Suhlik wanted her dead, she'd be dead. They had to know Mylomon would not rest until he found her.

So this was a trap and she was the bait.

The Suhlik wanted their foundling back.

Daisy surveyed the room. Four walls. No furniture,

no blanket or pillow. The floor and walls were made of a dense, spongy material. A sani unit and waste receptacle was in one corner. Water came from the other corner. No food. No warmth. A seam or seal for a door was not obvious. All four walls appeared perfectly smooth.

Daisy had nothing to do but wait. She curled into a ball, tucking in her hands and feet. Someone would come. They needed her alive so they would have to feed her and give her clothes, or a blanket. A blanket would be so good. At the very least, someone would come to gloat. The bad guys always did that.

* * *

STRONG HANDS GRABBED HER ROUGHLY UNDER THE armpits and lifted her off the floor. Daisy floundered, struggling to find her footing. The unseen person pulled her hair, yanking her head back. The Suhlik filled her vision, golden skin shimmering with delicate scales and a face so classically handsome it was unreal.

The Suhlik hissed words, her implanted translator chip slow to render the meaning. "Move, you ugly ape."

Daisy spat, hitting him on the cheek.

The male's eyes narrowed and his lips split into a grin. Row after row of sharp, needle-like teeth gleamed in the light. Monster. A true monster, the fairy tale kind that seduced innocents with pretty faces and promises and then gobbled them up.

She should have never called Mylo a monster. She apologized but now she truly regretted her words. She didn't mean them. He wasn't a monster. He was what the monsters had made him, yes, but he was also so much more.

"I'm not afraid of you," she said. "I know you need me alive."

The male delivered a swift punch to her stomach. Daisy doubled over, pulling her hair again before he released his grip and she fell to the floor.

"We need you alive, not pretty," the male said.

"Are you insane? Do not damage the female," a second male said.

Fantastic. More Suhlik. At least this one didn't want her damaged. Yet.

Daisy was pushed out of the cell, down a corridor and into a medical exam room. The male gave her a paper robe before stomping away. Designed for a larger frame, it hung off her.

She took in the room, not that there was much to take in. There was an exam table in the center. That was it. She knew she was meant to sit on the table, waiting for whatever the Suhlik planned to subject her to, but she couldn't bring herself to do it. She'd rather stand. Or sit on the floor. Anything but comply.

The door opened. A different Suhlik male entered, as ethereally beautiful as the previous. This one lacked a look of malice, which should have eased her worry but instead only served to unnerve her. This one had plans for her and she was pretty sure those plans were bad news.

He circled around her, examining her from all angles. He hissed, sounding almost like words. The implanted translator chip had a moment of lag while it rendered the hisses into an understandable language. "You're not what I expected."

Daisy opened her mouth for a devastatingly witty retort but a prick on her arm distracted her. "What the hell, man," she said, rubbing the afflicted spot.

The male inserted the lancet into a handheld device. "Hmm. You are not with child. Why are you not with child?"

"None of your damn business."

"Unfortunate. I hoped to have a specimen." He waved a second device over her from head to foot. "When the experiment returns, we will inseminate."

Daisy knocked the scanner away when he approached her. "What are you talking about? Where am I? Why am I here?"

"Hmm. Not the brightest star in the sky but what can you expect from a mutant."

"Mutant? I'm not—"

The Suhlik darted forward, pricking her again. This time Daisy's vision swam and her head grew fuzzy. Drugged. Fantastic. This day just—

She slumped to the floor.

Not unconscious, she was aware of everything the Suhlik male did. He picked her up and placed her on the table, strapping her down. Various needles drew blood. Daisy tried to look away, to flinch, to shout the most obscene insults she could muster, but her body refused to comply. She was helpless as the male went about his work.

At some point the realization that the male was a scientist or doctor drifted into her head. It was obvious but her thinker was on the fritz it seemed.

"Now what makes you so special, hmm?" The male

removed the paper robe and conducted a physical examination. Starting with her eyes, he shined a bright light and peered in. She tried to turn her head, to blink, anything to impede his progress. Elegant fingers shoved into her mouth, probing. She could bite. She wanted to bite. Her traitorous body did nothing.

The examination progressed from head to toe, his hands lifting and prodding every inch of her. He pried open her thighs and peered at her exposed sex but did not touch, instead promising an internal examining.

"Externally," the male said, "the subject is unremarkable. Internal scans reveal nothing of note. Perhaps a genetic analysis will divulge the little ape's secrets."

Daisy's voice was a gurgle in her throat.

The Suhlik cocked his head to one side. "Oh look, it speaks. Do you want to know why you are here?" He leaned in, face hovering over hers. "Because you are an aberration, little ape. Why is my wayward experiment able to breed with you? Hmm? I want to rip open those steaming guts of yours and get your eggs but we both know the Mahdfel can't reproduce in a test tube. Call it a design flaw on our part. So I'll keep your baby making parts inside you. For now."

The male spun and disappeared from her view, returning with a new device, a syringe with a very long needle. "I could still take a sampling. You Terrans have so many eggs that go to waste. The trauma would elevate the difficulty of impregnating you but the information I could gleam might be worth the risk. Choices, choices."

Another gurgle, this one closer to actual words.

"Shhh. Don't move or you'll hurt yourself."

The needle slid in, piercing through the soft layer of fat on her lower abdomen. Pain started a small prick then flared into a burn, growing in intensity. Her body wanted to convulse, to protest the deep invasion, but remained as immobile as ever.

"I had really hoped you'd be pregnant by now. We engineered a strong drive to breed into the Mahdfel. Their two primary functions: to fight and to fuck. So why hasn't our experiment been fucking you?" A clammy finger skimmed along the curve of mark-free neck. Another peer into her eyes. This times Daisy managed to blink. "No matter. My little experiment has a great deal of self-control. He may have suspected that I would want to study your wonderfully mutated genes so he fought against his base instincts, to protect you." A chuckle, smooth and golden and thoroughly evil. "How sweet."

"Know thissa trah-ph," Daisy slurred.

The male turned to his devices. He hit a button, presumably to increase the dosage. "Hmm. You burned through that sedative rather fast for such a small thing. Interesting. And yes, of course this is a trap. How else am I going to breed more teleporters?"

"Bree—" The sedative hit her, rendering her immobile.

The male shook his head. "Not bright at all. Yes, breed. I've been trying to engineer fertile teleporters for... seventy years now? Because engineering teleportation into soldiers individually is slow and expensive. The rejection rate is frightfully high. Imagine if they were simply born that way? But every one of my experiments have been frustratingly infertile. I even tried with a Terran female but I guess I'll never know how that one will turn out. Imagine my surprise when I learned that my lost experiment had a mate? A genetically compatible female?"

Daisy's memory spun back to conversations with Mylo, about how he expected to be alone, his surprise at finding her and his fear of rejection. He expected to be alone because all the other foundlings, the survivors of Suhlik experiments, were alone. The experiments fundamentally changed their genetic make-up.

"And I know my experiment is nothing special. He's not even the most gifted. He's just the one that got away. So *you* must be the special one in this equation."

Her. They wanted her.

"Why are you different? I will find out your secret. Mutation? Environmental factor? Don't worry. We're going to have a long time to get to know each other and thoroughly explore the subject. Now I'm going to implant a small device. I won't explain it because you wouldn't understand. Let's just say that if you leave this room, the device explodes. You're not going to like this."

Another tap of the device, a surge of a new drug, and Daisy blacked out.

MYLOMON

HE RAN THROUGH THE NIGHT. HE LEFT THE SUPPLIES,

only carrying his rifle, knife, and enough water and ration bars to fuel him. When dawn touched the horizon, he continued to run, only pausing for water and food. He ran past exhaustion but he was still not fast enough. Finally, near dusk, he arrived at the mountain.

His instinct told him to dash in, rip the beating heart out of every Suhlik unfortunate enough to encounter him and find his mate.

That was a foolish plan. They knew he would come. What choice did he have? His Daisy remained inside their stronghold. He would be overwhelmed with superior numbers. He would fail his mate. Unacceptable.

Devise another plan.

He could slip in. No door or wall could keep him out. Then, silent as a shadow and deadly as righteous vengeance, he could slit their throats and free his mate.

But these were the monsters who created him. Surely hellstone lined every wall in the facility, creating a cage for the those within and a barrier to those without.

There might be a gap in the hellstone. But that would be an obvious path to lead him into a trap. No.

He would fail his mate and get himself killed in his foolishness.

He needed to devise a good plan and not run in on instinct. Daisy had a tactical mind. She remained calm and assessed all available information. A pang of longing for his mate stabbed at his gut. It was more than her being useful. It was more than him needing to possess her, to stroke her hair and reassure himself of her safety.

He *missed* her and her chattering and her jokes and the way she sang softly when she walked.

What would Daisy recommend?

He closed his eyes and visualized her, hands on hips and giving him a look that implied he was an idiot. And he was being one, she'd say, because he thought he had to do this on his own.

His eyes flew open.

He was not alone.

He touched his communicator and hoped the *Judgment* was in range.

CHAPTER NINETEEN

DAISY

THE COLD DID NOT WAKE HER. THE COLD NEVER stopped and she never fell into a true sleep. Straps held her to the table. Wiggling her arms and legs, she determined there were straps at her feet, just above the knees, across her abdomen, which also caught her hands, and across her upper chest. She wasn't going anywhere.

Her neck *hurt*. Stiff, she attempted to turn her head. The muscles protested. Nope. Not moving today.

The bright overhead lights blinded her. The only

relief was to close her eyes, as poor a solution as that was.

Thunder rumbled.

No, scratch that. Not exactly thunder but definitely a rumble. Her table vibrated. Thunder didn't do that. Something was happening.

"Hey! Assholes! I'm freezing in here." She wiggled her fingers, trying to catch the edge of the straps. Maybe if she could free a hand...

Daisy didn't have a plan beyond irritating her captors, not that she expected them to set her free to get rid of a pest. Still, if she could extract some annoyance that would be a small measure of justice.

A dark shadow fell over her.

Crap. Now she'd done it.

She didn't want to open her eyes. All her resolve to be a thorn in the Suhlik's side vanished. They were here and they were going to hurt her.

What was she going to do? Lay there with her eyes closed, whimpering in fear?

Screw that and screw them.

Daisy opened her eyes.

A dark face hovered over hers. The beloved sharp

profile and aggressive horns warmed her heart. My-lomon.

"Female, remain still. You are safe." His deep, rich voice surrounded her as he undid the straps.

"I know I am. You're here." He found her. Relief flooded Daisy. She knew he knew find her. The worry replaced relief. "This is a trap. They're expecting you."

"I know. The clan is here keeping them occupied."

He moved to lift her off the table. She laid a hand on his arm to stop him. "The male in charge, he knew you. You. From when you were a child."

Mylomon growled. "I remember him. My brothers will take care of him."

"Don't you want vengeance or something? Confront your Darth Vader?"

"You are more important. He is the past. You are my future."

It could have been stress or hormones but at that moment, she loved him completely.

He lifted her, cradling him to her chest.

"Ouch!"

Mylomon frozen. "Female?"

"They put something in me. A bomb. I can't leave the room, he told me, or it will detonate."

He returned her to the table. "We do not have much time. Tell me what I must do."

"You bring a surgeon? Kalen?"

"No. I brought no medics and I do not believe there is time for one to arrive."

"Okay." She took a deep breath. "I'm going to talk you through this. First, we need to determine if he actually put something in me. That might have been just talk. Get that scanner," she pointed to a shelf.

She turned on the device and instructed Mylomon on how to use it. There was a device, implanted on a vertebra just below the base of her skull. Fan-fucking-tastic.

"Any idea the type of detonation it uses?" she asked.

"Proximity."

"Can you reach in a pluck it out?" Yay for mutant powers.

He studied the image. "I fear damaging a nerve. I could cripple you."

"Hmm." Daisy enlarged the image. "Humans keep their nerves inside the vertebra. Our bones aren't as... sturdy as yours but it works the same way. The device seems to be located on the cervical spine. C2. In the facet joint, which explains why I can't turn my head."

She looked up at him, a smile on her face. His expression was blank. He did not follow. "That's good. That's the cartilage between." His expression remained blank. "It's miles away from the nerves. Even if we do a sloppy job, I'll be fine. Movement might not be so great but it's not great now." She hoped Kalen would be able to repair any significant damage from extraction.

"I am unsure, female."

Daisy patted his arm. "I know this is a tough call, but I can't leave here if this *thing* is in me."

"I do not know what—"

She squeezed his hand and smiled reassuringly at him. "You got this. I trust you."

He huffed. "I can sink my fingers in and root around. You will not like the sensation. And I will not be able to see what I am touching." He could teleport through object, not see through them.

"We'll set up the scanner so you can see what you're touching." She shivered at the idea. He would be touching *her*. Inside her. "I'll need something to block the pain but not put me under. Can you read Suhlik?" He nodded. She rattled off what drug she would prefer and what would suffice. He found it quickly.

"I might not be able to speak after I take this. Do you know what to do?"

He pressed his lips to hers. "You are my heart, wife. I will bring you through this."

She filled a hypospray and injected herself on the side of her neck. Immediately a numbing sensation spread, separating her head from her body. So curious.

She either fell to the table or he pushed her down. Daisy wasn't sure. She was horizontal on her stomach. Mylomon adjusted the scanner above. "Are you ready?" he asked.

Unable to reply, a warm, tingling sensation spread at the back of her head but otherwise she felt nothing. She knew she'd feel it in the morning.

Seconds ticked by. She counted his breaths. Slow. Measure. Calm. No panic. The steady rhythm of his breathing gave her confidence.

"Finished." He pushed away the scanner and helped her sit up. The room swam and she was unable to keep herself from tipping over. Next to her on the table was a small chip, not bigger than a fingernail, coated in blood. Her blood.

Wrapped in a sheet, Mylomon cradled her in his

arms, the safest spot in the universe. She wanted to tell him that but her throat refused to cooperate. At least her respiration remained normal.

Outside the operating theater, warriors filled the halls with shouts and blaster fire. Smoke burned her eyes. She needed to cough but could not, a terrible tickling sensation grew at the base of her throat. Seeran spotted Mylomon and provided cover, allowing him to exit the corridor. Having obtained their objective, the clan fell back as a unit and exited the building.

Outside, cold air hit her face, bringing tears to her eyes. She coughed, throat heaving. Mylomon rubbed her back while her chest burned to expel the smoke.

"I want this mountain leveled," Paax shouted. "Not a single stone standing. Make it happen."

Mylomon hustled her onto a shuttle. The comforting sound of engines replaced the cacophony of battle. A fresh set of flex-armor replaced the bedsheet.

"Ready to go home?" he asked.

"Home is with you," she managed to croak out.

CHAPTER TWENTY

DAISY

MEDICAL WAS THE FIRST, NON-NEGOTIABLE STOP. While Kalen gave her a full scan, Mylomon paced and growled. He was no help at all.

"I'm fine," she said. The local anesthesia had worn off. Movement returned to her neck. She was a little stiff but that was nothing unexpected.

"That is for me to say, Nurse Vargas," Kalen said in a bored tone. Bored had to be good, right? Bored meant everything was fine. If she picked up a parasite or an alien virus, he'd sound mildly concerned?

Maybe peeved. She studied her brother-in-law's scowling face. Definitely peeved.

"Ankle tendonitis. Levator scapula is inflamed. Surface abrasions on the epidermis," Kalen finally concluded, applying a warm gel to the scrapes. "Your mate did a poor job of protecting you."

"I think he did fine," Daisy said, totally not admiring the way Mylomon's muscular form stalked through Medical. Totally not checking him out.

Kalen pressed a hypospray to her arm. "What's that?" she asked.

"A stimulant."

"I don't need a stimulant. I'm half asleep."

"Exactly."

Meridan arrived before Daisy could tear in Kalen about his brusk bedside manner. Her sister had a child in tow.

That was new.

The girl, aged somewhere between the age of six and seven, had a stuffed bear on each arm. Her head was shaved but starting to grow out. A dark fuzz covered her scalp. She dashed around medical like she was being chased. Kalen and Meridan both ignored the running and occasionally prompted her not to climb the delicate equipment.

The sisters exchanged hugs and tears. Finally, Meridan pulled away and said, "You stink. Like really stink. Let's get you cleaned up."

"I will leave you with your sister," Mylomon said. "I have duties I must see to."

The smile fell from Daisy's face. Nothing changed after all. Duty to the clan came before everything, even her. Would she love her warrior if he was any less dedicated? Mylo wouldn't be Mylo if he had the inclination to play hooky from work. Still, it hurt to know she was always second. "Oh. Okay. When will you be home?"

Mylomon lifted her chin and searched her eyes. Sometimes it felt like he could read her mind. "You are my home and I am never far. I shall return soon."

Meridan waited until they were in the corridor before the questioning began. "So?"

Her sister was devastating in her simplicity. She knew Daisy would be unable to resist such a broad prompt.

"So yourself," she replied.

"Don't give me that. Where are your questions? I know you're bursting to get them out," Meridan said. Which meant Merri was dying to get the scoop from Daisy.

"Oh my god, Merri. Where did the kid come from? She's cute, don't get me wrong. What happened on the planet surface? You won't believe what happened to us! I have so many things to tell you."

"The kid is Estella. She's our foundling. Our daughter, now."

They arrived at her quarters, which gave Daisy time to formulate a response. A foundling. Just like Mylomon. "She was in that research facility?"

"Yes."

"And Kalen accepts—"

"He didn't have a choice."

"I can't believe you found a kid and just adopted her."

"She adopted us, not the other way around."

Daisy laughed. Her sister, who never expected to have children, now had a hyperactive six-year-old. "That sounds so fantastic. I'm an aunt! I hope she likes meddling because I have a feeling that I'm the meddling kind of auntie. How does that sound, Estella?"

The child in question climbed onto the sofa and started to bounce. "Did she lose her shoes somewhere?"

"We're working on shoes," Meridan sighed. "She's never worn them before. Bathing was a battle."

"Speaking of. Someone told me I stank."

"I'll wait out here. Anything I need to keep out of the reach of children past their bedtime?"

"Stay out of the knife room," Daisy called as she entered the cleansing room. She heard a small voice shouting about knives and Meridan repeating "no." Being an aunt was a blast.

Bathed, dressed in clean clothes and feeling like a person again, Meridan announced her intentions to feed her.

"I'm fine. I just want to sleep." Bed, a real bed with pillows and a mountain of snuggly blankets, had the allure of a siren's song.

"Nonsense. You've had what? Ration bars for days? Come eat a real meal with the people who love you."

Everyone except her husband, she thought bitterly. "Fine. I require caffeine, sugar and a lot of grease."

"I've got you covered. So how are things between you and... I know you were unhappy before all this mess happened."

"Good, actually. Surprisingly." As she said the words, she knew she spoke true but that would fail to satisfy her sister's curiosity. "We had a lot of time to talk."

"Talk. Right," Meridan said with a wink.

Ugh. Sisters.

They walked past the mess hall. Estella ran down the corridor and back, circling them before darting off again. "That was the mess. Aren't we stopping?"

"Not today."

"Merri, I'm too tired for games. Where are you taking me?"

"Hush. Enjoy the surprise."

Meridan brought her to the orchard. A low table with cushions was set on the grass. A crowd milled. She recognized Vox and Kalen. Estella ran toward Kalen with her arms fully extended and launched herself at him. He caught her with a laugh. Mercy rested on a cushion and the warlord rubbed her lower back. There were a few unknown faces in the crowd but that didn't matter. She searched for the only face that mattered.

"Surprise!" Meridan exclaimed, draping an arm

over her shoulder. "Well, aren't you going to say something?"

"Hmm? Yeah, sounds great," Daisy said, distracted. Mylomon came toward her. He wore his normal uniform of loose fitting togs and no shirt. Not that she minded. Not at all.

"I required guidance in the concept of date night," he said.

Her hand flew to her mouth and she bite down on a knuckle. She wasn't going to cry. She'd survived being stranded on an alien planet, chased by a strange armadillo-bear, and kidnapped by a Suhlik mad scientist. She was too tough to cry over the sweetest, most thoughtful male in the universe.

"Wife?" he asked in a murmur, his hand on her neck.

"I'm good. I'm just really, really happy."

"Terrans cry when they are sad. And now they cry when they are happy?"

"We cry a lot," she said with a sniff. "This is wonderful."

The aroma of everything good and delicious wafted toward her. Her stomach rumbled.

"You hunger. Let me feed you, mate."

She nodded, too hungry to protest.

Mylomon sat Daisy directly in his lap. Dinner was Terran: spaghetti and meatballs with garlic bread. He fed her the meatballs and bites of bread with his bare hands but she insisted on using a fork for the noodles. "I appreciate the sentiment but this is messy."

The Mahdfel males poked politely at their plates of noodles. Too many carbohydrates for their palate. Estella followed Kalen's lead, pushing around the spaghetti and sighing forlornly. It was strangely adorable watching a six-year-old throw a tantrum over food but even better watching the grown men throw the same tantrum.

"I like these meatballs," Vox declared loudly, holding forth a meatball impaled on his fork. "It is like consuming the eye of my enemies." Then he popped the entire meatball in his mouth, grinning as he chewed theatrically.

"You don't even do that," Meridan said, completely missing Estella popping a meatball into her own mouth.

After the meal, the warlord approached. "I'll listen to your report," he said, settling on a cushion next to

Mylomon. Daisy moved to her feet but a hand on her shoulder encouraged her to remain.

"Stay, mate. This is as much your mission as mine." Mylomon gave a brief outline of events, elaborating when Paax asked for details.

"Hmm." The warlord stroked his chin. "The Suhlik claimed the girl child was to be bred?"

Mylomon wrapped his arms around Daisy, protectively.

Paax waved away his unspoken concerns with a hand. "I'm not interested in making more teleporters. Two is more than enough."

"Is she a teleporter, too?" Daisy asked. She watched Estella feed "eyeballs" to Kalen and Meridan.

"Yes. Perhaps more talented than Mylomon."

Her husband huffed. Daisy patted him on the shoulder consolingly. No one liked to be replaced with a younger model. "That remains to be seen," he said.

"Funny you should say that," Paax said. "I'm restructuring your duties. You will be responsible for the training and education of the girl."

Mylomon nodded but Daisy groaned. Another responsibility to keep her mate away. "You can't," she said. "Estella is just a child. She can't be an assassin."

"She is a child with a powerful ability. She needs to learn control. Without control she endangers herself and the clan. As for being an assassin," Paax said, eyes drifting toward Meridan and back to Daisy. "Kalen's female has forbidden it and my mate has forbidden me from stealing the childhood of a particular little girl."

"But you will turn her into a weapon, just not that *particular* weapon." Not a question. And where was all this attitude coming from? You didn't speak to the warlord that way and expect to walk away.

A grin lifted the corners of Paax's mouth, exposing just the hint of fang. "Kalen has claimed Estella as his child. She is Mahdfel now. All Mahdfel children train as warriors. It is our way."

Daisy relaxed, leaning back against Mylomon's chest. Meridan most likely had this argument already. She wouldn't gain new ground with the warlord. She'd have to trust Merri's judgment.

"I also want you to delegate your duties to Seeran," Paax said.

"The security chief?" Mylomon asked.

"Yes. He is energetic, ambitious and its time he be a pain in your ass instead of mine. If you find yourself pressed for time between your new responsibilities," his eyes drifted to Daisy again, "then conscript more hands."

Daisy turned to her husband, eyes wide. "Does that mean you get minions, sweetie?"

Mylomon nodded. The times were changing after all.

"There is one more thing, sir," Mylomon said, turning back to the warlord. "About breeding."

Paax cocked his head to one side. "The Suhlik wanted to examine your mate and determine if she could conceive."

"Yes. They had doubts if she could conceive."

"The genetic test is always correct. She is compatible."

Daisy was uncomfortable with the way the two males talked about her like she wasn't even there.

"Perhaps. But will she be able to conceive? To carry to term?"

"Hmm. Yes. I could examine your mate—"

"I'd rather find out the old fashioned way, thank you," Daisy said.

The warlord nodded. "Of course. We will need to monitor any fetus for complications. And we do not know if your mate's unique ability is an inheritable trait. If so, we do not know when that ability would manifest itself in the unborn."

Daisy placed a protective hand over her stomach. A teleporting baby was a terrifying idea. A teleporting, underdeveloped baby more so. Unable to survive on it's own, her child might unwittingly damage itself. And she'd be helpless to stop it.

"We would need to monitor constantly. And determine a way to contain the unborn child for his own safety."

"Hellstone?" Mylomon suggested.

Paax stroked his chin. "The Suhlik implanted capsules of hellstone in Estella to control her movements. That could be a solution."

"No," Daisy said. "You're not implanting anything in me." One device was more than enough. "How about a belt?" She moved her hand across her stomach to demonstrate where a belt would sit. "A hellstone belt? Would that protect our son?"

Mylomon's face lit up when she said the word "son". She melted a little inside at his excitement for their future.

"That could work. I'll have the engineers work on

it," the warlord said before returning to the smiling embrace of his mate.

"Our son?" Mylomon asked. The smile on his face was so happy and so damn sexy, her knees wobbled.

"Well, you know, one day." Her words were cool but the truth was she wanted to jump him right at that moment and start making that son. She didn't care who saw. Mylomon was her abomination. Her monster. Hers.

The lights in the orchard dimmed and the windows turned white. Images flickered across the screen. Mylomon leaned down, breath hot against the shell of her ear. "I still think films are a waste of time."

"Shh," she said, trying to ignore the way he nuzzled her neck.

"I can think of activities I'd much rather be doing." His teeth grazed the sensitive skin where her neck joined her shoulder. He bit down, applying just enough pressure to catch her attention.

Her breath stopped and her back went straight. "Seriously? Now?"

"Haven't we waited long enough?" he murmured. His tongue lathed the spot where he would mark his claim. He did not play fair. So not fair. They could sneak out. The lights were dimmed. Every pair of eyes was watching the film, not them.

"What are you waiting for," she answered.

Mylomon growled in response, sweeping her up and tossing her over his shoulder. Daisy thrashed her legs. "Oh my God, put me down."

"Female, quiet yourself."

"Everyone is looking!" Vox hooted his encouragement. Embarrassment flooded through her. So much for sneaking out unawares.

"Good. The clan needs to see how a male pleases his female." His hand swatted her playfully on the bottom.

Daisy thought she might die from mortification if she wasn't so turned. "Are you going to stand there and brag about it or are you going to do something about it?"

The clan laughed cheerfully as Mylomon carried his wife to their quarters.

CHAPTER TWENTY-ONE

MYLOMON

ONCE IN THEIR QUARTERS, MYLOMON LOWERED Daisy, her body sliding down his until her feet touched the ground. Her touch set him on fire but he needed to remain in control for a little while longer.

"Are you well?" he asked.

She nodded. "The doc checked me out."

"Tired?"

"I'm fine."

"Sore?"

She cocked her head to one side. "What is this about? I'm fine."

"I do not wish to rush you into—"

"Oh my God, Mylo," she said, stretching up on her tiptoes and grabbing his horns. She pulled them down roughly. The curious twin sensations of pleasure and pain ran down his spine.

He did not mind her rough touch.

"I want this. I want *you*," she said, planting a kiss on his lips. "I know you love me. You've been telling —*showing*— me but I didn't do a good job of listening." Her eyes searched his. Fingers still gripping his horns, she commanded his attention. "You know I love you, right?"

"It seems too impossible to be true."

"Stars, you are the sweetest idiot."

"I am what I am."

Her hands fell away from his horns, releasing the sensual pressure. She began to unfasten his armor. While his mate had time to be examined by Kalen, shower and change into fresh clothes, he still wore the same filthy armor. "I need to shower."

"No," she said sharply, swatting him lightly on the shoulder. His dark eyes softened. "We can shower after. Together."

Agreement rumbled in his chest. He approved of her suggestion.

"Until then, my husband is wearing too many clothes." Her hands returned to unfastening his armor. As much as he relished her attention, the clasps refused to cooperate with her.

"Let me, wife," he said. The clasps opened easily and the armor plating fell off. It was good to get out of the stolen Suhlik armor. It was even better to strip for his wife. Finally, he stood naked for her perusal.

Daisy sucked in her breath. "I don't know how you did it, but you got hotter."

He raised an eyebrow. "You told me I was gorgeous."

She nodded, failing to sense his playful tone. "Hot and gorgeous. And mine." She reached out to lightly touch a pectoral and drew her hand back quickly. "May I touch you, husband?"

He nodded. "If you do not, you will break my heart."

"Can't have that." Her hands skimmed his chest. Fingers traced over the ridges on his abdomen. Her fingers went lower still, to the V of his pelvic muscles and then lower still. He held his breath, waiting for her warm hands to brush against his hardening cock or circle its girth but at the last moment her fingers diverted to his hips. Her touch was maddeningly delicious and he wouldn't trade it for anything in the universe.

She cupped his ass, gave it a firm squeeze and sighed. "Stars, no one has the right to have a booty like that."

"It pleases you?"

"I was staring at it while we hiked across the tundra and all could think about was sinking my teeth into that booty."

"That's a good thing?" he asked for clarification.

"It's a great thing." Her hands continued to journey north, up his back, tracing along his spine, and finally her arms settled around his neck. She leaned in close to the base of his neck, breath hot against his skin.

"May I lick you, husband?" Her fingers traced the cords of his neck.

"If it pleases you, wife," he managed to say.

Her tongue, her hot, perfect tongue, licked the cords of his neck. A shiver of delight worked through him. It took all his control not to push her down to the floor and sink into her hot, perfect core.

"Husband, may I—"

"Wife," he interrupted. "The answer is yes. This body is yours. You may touch, lick, kiss, caress, nibble, bite, and whatever you please with it. But if I do not touch you soon, I will explode."

She chuckled.

At him. Him. The dreaded assassin. The necessary tool. The abomination that made full grown warriors nervous.

He did not believe it was possible to love her any more than he did.

His wife moved to lift the hem of her dress. "Allow me," he said. The dress slipped over her head easily, the silky fabric making a slight whisper as it moved over her skin. He discarded the garment, leaving it in a heap on the floor. She stepped out of her shoes. He tugged down her panties and removed her bra. She was bare before him.

Daisy was beautiful. Her golden hair tumbled over one shoulder, onto the heavy globes of her breasts. Tight pink nipples invited him to suck. Her belly was soft, as a female should be, and her hips were made for a warrior's hold.

A slight blush came over her and she lifted an

arm to cover her breasts. Mylomon stopped her. There were too few things of genuine beauty in the universe to go covering up such a wonder.

He had seen her naked form before. He had licked her sweet cunt and drank her juices as she came on his mouth. "You only get lovelier."

Her blush deepened. "You're only saying that because you're going to get some."

"I say that because it's true." A finger under her chin lifted her face to his.

The kiss started light but his intensity matched her need and it deepened. He lifted her, her legs wrapping around his waist. He stumbled toward the sofa before falling down. Daisy giggled. It was the sweetest sound, her face pressed to his neck, laughing at his lack of grace.

Her laughter filled him with hope and light. She laughed at him because she was not scared of him. And if she was not scared of him, perhaps her words of love were true. She really did love an abomination like him. She had told him many times. Had shown him in many ways but he did not believe her.

Until now.

"I was wrong," he said, dazed. "I love you more now than ever."

"Words, words, words," she said between kisses to his brow, nose and lips. "Show me."

He positioned her over his throbbing cock. The head brush along the length of her. She was wet. He knew he should spend time getting her ready to take all of him. Lick her. Opening her with his fingers. But his control was thin and Daisy didn't protest. She planted her hands on his shoulders and rubbed herself against the head of his cock, eyes closed in pleasure.

Hands on her hips, he lowered her onto his member. Tightness and searing heat enveloped the head. He surged upwards, driving all the way in. Daisy gasped above him. "Did I hurt you?" he asked.

"No," she said, her voice near a moan. Her hands shot up from his shoulders and grabbed his horns firmly. He wasn't sure which was more pleasurable. Her hips rocking back and forth, working the length of him. Or the sensual pressure at the base of his horns. To have both at the same time was mind breaking.

"Don't you dare stop, husband."

Joined now they moved together. His world

narrowed to his beautiful wife in his arms. She was improbable, impossible in so many ways. It was improbable to find a female compatible with his genetic mutations. Improbable that she desired him. Improbable that she continued to desire him after he tried to push her way. Impossible for him to go on without her in his life. Without her smiles. Without her fearless laughter.

His fangs lengthened. He neared his climax and it was time to mark his mate, to claim her properly. "Daisy," he said.

Her eyes flew opened. "You said my name."

"Daisy, my love, I'm going to claim you now. I need you to come with me." His hand worked her clit, sending uncontrollable shivers through her. She was close. He could feel her grip tighten and ripple around him. Her pulled her in, tilted her head to the side to expose her delicate neck. Finally, at their peak, he let go.

His teeth sank into the curve where her neck joined her shoulder. The coppery taste of her Terran blood flooded his mouth but his jaw would not release. Not yet. The mark needed to be deep enough for everyone to know that this female, this perfect female, belonged to him. After a minute, his fangs retreated.

He washed the wound with his tongue. Part of him, the ancient feral part of his brain, knew his saliva sped along the healing process.

She remained still under him while he licked the wound.

Satisfied, he rolled to one side, bringing her with him. She nuzzled under his arm. The steady rhythm of her heartbeat created the sweetest music. His mate. His heart.

"Do you think we will be able to have children?" she asked.

"Yes," he said with certainty.

"How do you know that? What if the baby doesn't... stay put? Inside my womb?"

He rubbed circles on her arms, enjoying the feel of her silky skin under his. "I know you are a miracle, Daisy Vargas. Your love is a miracle. Your laughter is a gift. You are my future and I do not worry because you are with me."

She turned her face into his chest but he could feel her smile. "You are the sweetest, scariest damn thing I've ever seen and you're *mine*. My superhero."

"Not your monster?"

"No, sweetie. Actions make a monster and all I've

seen from you is one hundred percent hero business." Her wonderful, delicate, perfect hand traced lazy circles on his chest. "Why don't you have any tattoos?"

Mylomon took a deep breath. "I had no rank. No family. No point."

Her fingers traced an invisible pattern stretching across his collarbone. "Hmm. I'm getting better at reading you. Now how about you tell me the truth this time, husband."

"Clever female. I was an assassin." He paused. She waited. "The tattoos glow when we become emotional. A glowing assassin is a poor tool."

A smile spread across her face. "A glow-in-the-dark Mylo." Then, "So that's why you won't wear a damn shirt."

He cocked his head to one side, ready to listen to her deductions.

Her laughter started a quiet giggle, growing louder and more raucous until she was red in the face and couldn't look at him. She rolled away, trying to catch her breath.

"Are you well?"

"Yes." Her shoulders shook with laughter. "It's just... the funniest damn thing you've ever done. And it's such a long con." She turned toward him, eyes bright. "All those muscle-headed warriors ragging on you about having 'no family, no name, no honor'." Her voice switched to a mocking gruff tone. "And it was *practical*. And then you strut around like shirtless bar-barian, flaunting it. You could have a tattoo now but you won't because you like to make them nervous. That's so spiteful." The laughter came back. "Stars, you can be a dick. I love it."

"My difference makes my clan uncomfortable. So I embrace that difference." He admired the way her mind made quick connections. She was correct. The reasons were originally practical. Some in his clan would shame him so he forged that shame into a tool for agitation.

"We call that 'owning it'."

Her laughter was melodious. Miraculous. It wrapped around his heart, settling in for a lifetime. "I believe I will get a small tattoo. Here." He tapped a spot above his heart. "A small flower."

Her laughter stilled but her smile remained. "Sounds absolutely terrifying."

It was past time for Mylomon to put that shadowy assassin behind him. "I have much to celebrate. My clan needs to admire my rank, my miracle of a female and my growing family." He gave her ass a slap for emphasis, before rolling onto his back. He pulled her over him, settling her above his hips and hardening cock.

Her eyes went wide. "Again?"

His wife was a miracle that pulled a monster from the shadows. She was better than he deserved and he would spend the rest of his days worshipping the miracle that was her.

EPILOGUE

VOX

"**W**HAT THE BLAZING STARS DID YOU DO TO MY baby?" The female's voice was muffled as half her torso dangled inside the guts of the fighter jet. Clanking tools and the general noise of the hanger drowned out the string of expletives directed at the clumsy pilot.

Which would be him.

But he really couldn't think about that because underneath the smell of metal, grease and fuel was something like honey. Something just for him.

His mate. His female.

Finally.

"I brought her back in one piece," he managed to say.

The mechanic snorted and crawled out of the engine. "If you call this one piece. Tell Paax that repairing experimental equipment is not high on my priority list."

She was stunning. And filthy. Stunningly filthy. His female was pleasingly thick and strong. Grease marred her pale complexion. A stained cloth covered her head and held back vivid red hair. Freckles scattered across the bridge of her nose like stars. He needed to reach out and map each one; discover new constellations on her glorious body. He always did like freckles on Terran females.

"Hello? Earth to Fly Boy?" She tapped a wrench against the metal hull of the fighter. "I swear, they make you pretty but not too bright."

Vox grinned. His female thought he was pretty.

"Stars," she said. "You're him, aren't you?"

Thank you for reading!

I hope you enjoyed Mylomon. Vox is up next but not until the spring. He's just going to have to wait a hot minute.

Until then, if you enjoyed the story, please leave a review. If you found a typo, let me know at Nancey@ Menurapress.com. I'll get right on it.

Stay in the loop with my latest releases, freebie and special offers.

Join Nancey's newsletter
http://eepurl.com/b_NJyr

Are you a
STARR HUNTRESS?

Do you love to read sci fi romance about strong, independent women and the sexy alien males who love them?

Starr Huntress is a coalition of the brightest Starrs in romance banding together to explore uncharted territories.

If you like your men horny—maybe literally—and you're equal opportunity skin color—because who doesn't love a guy with blue or green skin?—then join us as we dive into swashbuckling space adventure, timeless romance, and lush alien landscapes.

Sign up for the Starr Huntress newsletter to get the very latest in releases, promos, giveaways and freebies:
http://eepurl.com/b_NJyr
Facebook: facebook.com/StarrHuntress/
Twitter: @StarrHuntress

Claimed by the Alien Prince

Prince Aster didn't believe in "mates" or other bed-time stories...until he sensed Evie's curious scent. The curvy human woman with curly brown hair and caramel skin is nothing like he expected—but someone unique and strange. This alpha alien must claim her and take her in every way.

Evie can't deny her attraction to the big blue alien 'man', or their chemistry—but his mate? Can she leave everyone and everything behind for this towering, muscular stranger from another world? His sky blue skin glows where they touch and it excites her in a passionate new way. Does she have a choice—or is it her destiny?

Be the first to know about new releases! No spam, just free promos and new stuff.

Join Nancey's newsletter
http://eepurl.com/b_NJyr

If you found a typo or a gigantic plot hole, drop me a line at Nanceycumm@gmail.com or @Nanceycumms on the tweets. I got the plot spackle ready to go.

Additional Titles

Warriors of Sangrin

Paax

Kalen

Mylomon

Vox

Korven's Fire (with Juno Wells)

Ragnar (with Juno Wells)

Delivered to the Aliens

Alpha Aliens of Fremm

Claimed by the Alien Prince

Bride of the Alien Prince

Alien Warrior's Mate

Alien Rogue's Price

Submitting to Monsters

The Lady of the Lake Monster
The Return of the Lady of the Lake Monster
The Lake Monster's Education

About Nancey

I am an unapologetic nerd. Time travel, space opera, superheroes, tabletop games, fountain pens and video games where you beat up robots, I love it all. I write the type of fun, fast and flirty books I want to read, featuring plucky heroines, wickedly charming heroes, and plenty of steamy, fun sex. Hopefully you want to read them to.

I live in an old house with my husband and two cats that have complaints with management. I try to wear pants as little as possible.

52372441R00172